LOVE'S ANSWER

LOVE'S MAGIC BOOK 8

BETTY MCLAIN

Copyright (C) 2019 Betty McLain

Layout design and Copyright (C) 2019 by Creativia

Published 2019 by Creativia (www.creativia.org)

Edited by Marilyn Wagner

Cover art by Cover Mint

This book is a work of fiction. Names, characters, places, and incidents are the product of the author's imagination or are used fictitiously. Any resemblance to actual events, locales, or persons, living or dead, is purely coincidental.

All rights reserved. No part of this book may be reproduced or transmitted in any form or by any means, electronic or mechanical, including photocopying, recording, or by any information storage and retrieval system, without the author's permission.

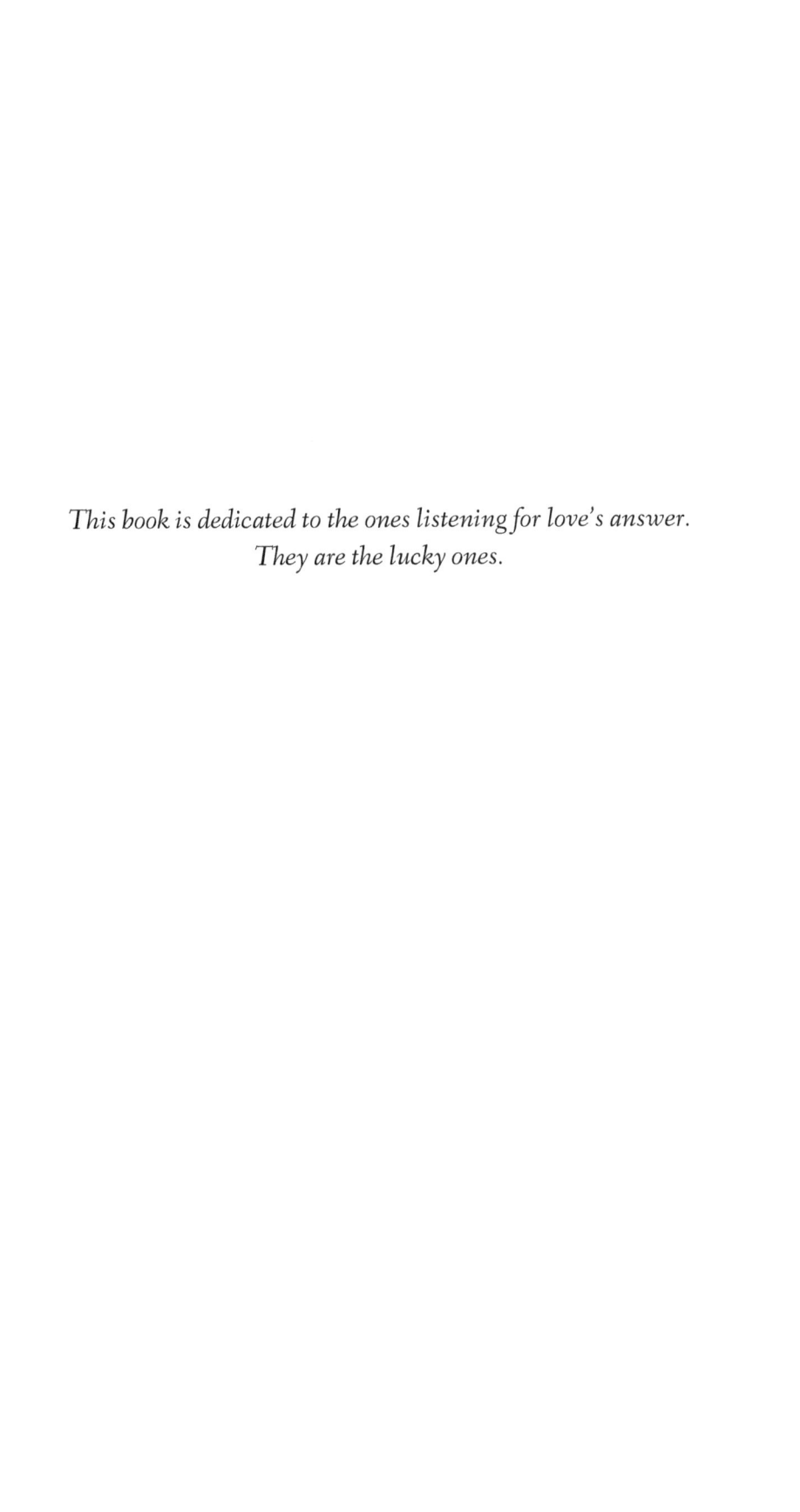

*This book is dedicated to the ones listening for love's answer.
They are the lucky ones.*

CHAPTER 1

Lilly Hemp stopped working on the flowers and looked around. This year's flowers were doing well. All of the flowers were blooming, and the bright colors were beautiful. She was working on gathering a bunch of the flowers, ready to harvest. D. D.'s Flower Shop in Sharpville, placed a large order for an upcoming wedding. Jed Hillard and Marissa Camp ordered the flowers to decorate the church. Their wedding was only a week away, and there was a lot of excitement in Sharpville. They were a very popular couple.

Lily knew Jed from school, but she did not know Marissa. Lily had not been out and around very much the last three years. She mostly let her brother handle meeting people and making deliveries. She had a hard time associating with people since the car accident three years ago destroyed her world.

Her husband, Mark, and her two-year-old daughter, Sue, had gone along with her mom and dad when they went to Sharpville to make a delivery. Their car was hit by a drunk driver. Everyone was killed.

Lily had been at home, sick with a cold, and her world had come apart when the deputy sheriff had shown up with the devastating news. Even though he was equally affected, her brother, Doug, took care of all the arrangements, and tried to help Lily, who was almost comatose with grief. She spent most of her time curled up on her bed, crying and clutching Sue's baby blanket.

Lily had finally stirred herself, much to Doug's relief, and started working with the flowers again. It seemed to help her being outside working in the flower beds. She even went a few days at a time when she did not feel like curling into a ball and crying her eyes out. So many things around the place reminded her of Sue.

"You are going to have to make this delivery tomorrow," said Doug at supper. "I have a buyer coming to see some horses." Doug raised horses on their farm and sold them to the rodeo crowd.

Lily looked at him hard to see if he was up to something. He didn't say anything else, just kept eating. Lily shrugged. "Okay," she said.

When Doug finished eating and went outside, he grinned with relief. He had been trying for a while to get Lily out of the house and around people. He was worried about her turning into a recluse. It would be good for her to get out and resume life.

Lily went to check on the flowers. They were in a cool storage box to preserve them until they could be delivered. They were all doing okay. She went to gather a few extra, just in case. She had a special van to deliver the flowers in. It was equipped with a cool box to keep the flowers fresh and D. D.'s also had a cool box to keep them in until needed. She would wait until morning to load the van. She went inside and washed her hands and started to prepare supper. She was a little apprehensive about tomorrow, but overall, she was still so numb she didn't think too much about it.

D. D., short for Danielle Denise, met Lily when she came to deliver the flowers. Between the two of them they soon had the flowers transferred from the van to storage in the flower shop. Lily decided to stop and eat before she headed for home. She also had to stop by the grocery store. Doug had given her a list of things to pick up while she was in town. She went by the grocery store first. She had no worries about things spoiling before she could get them home since she could use the cool storage in the van.

After loading up her groceries, Lily decided to stop at Danny's and pick up a hamburger. When she went in, the place was more crowded than she expected. She spotted an empty table and headed to it. After sitting down, she noticed a mirror displayed on the table. The waitress came up and distracted her before she could read the display.

Lily ordered her hamburger and coke. She sat back to wait for her order. Lily glanced around but didn't see anyone she recognized. Lily looked back at the mirror. She read what it said. "True love," she whispered. "How can I see true love in this mirror when my true love lies buried underneath an angel in the cemetery?" All of a sudden, the mirror showed a man's face in the mirror. Lily glanced behind her to see if anyone was behind her. No one was there. She looked back at the mirror. She shook her head. "No," she moaned. "It can't be."

She started to stand. The waitress came with her order. "Fix it to go," said Lily. She looked at the girl at the table next to her. "You asked the mirror a question. You can't blame the mirror if you don't like the answer." the girl said.

"You don't understand," said Lily. "He can't be my true love. My true love is dead."

"I don't know the answer. I only know the mirror is never wrong," said the girl.

"It is this time," said Lily. The waitress came back with her order and Lily gave her some money and hurried out. She wanted to be as far from the mirror as she could get.

Lily decided she was in no shape to be driving, so she headed for the park. She sat on a bench in the park and drank her coke. She couldn't eat her hamburger. Her stomach was rolling with tension. She looked at the children's playground next to the park and felt tears come into her eyes.

As she watched the children playing, a man came into the park. He had a little boy about two years old with him. They were walking through the park on their way to the children's playground. When they started to pass her, the man looked at her and smiled. He stopped smiling when he saw the tears in her eyes.

"Do you need help?" he asked. Lily shook her head. She was too choked up to talk. The little boy patted her on the knee and smiled at her. Lilly smiled back. He was a precious little boy. Sue had been just his age when she lost her. The man sat on the bench beside her and pulled the boy into his lap.

"I'm Samuel and this little monster is Sam," he said smiling at Sam. "I don't know too many people in Sharpville, yet. Sam and I just moved here a short time ago." Sam grinned at him.

"I'm Lily and I grow flowers on a farm west of here. I just came into town with a delivery. I stopped at Danny's for a hamburger before heading home and sat at a table with a mirror on it. It showed me a man who wasn't in the room. I was so upset I just got my hamburger and left."

"Ah, you looked in the magic mirror," said Samuel. Lily looked at him, startled. "You know about the mirror?" she asked.

"Yes, Crystal, at Sam's daycare, and I saw each other through the mirror. She was looking in the magic mirror, and I was at another mirror," said Samuel.

"Did you two get together?" asked Lily.

"We are still working on it," said Samuel.

"Who did you see in the mirror?" asked Sam.

"I don't know. He was a stranger. I wasn't looking for true love. My love died when my daughter and husband were killed three years ago," said Lily.

"I'm sorry for your loss. I know how hard it is to lose a child," said Samuel.

"Did you lose a child?" asked Lily.

"Sam here was kidnapped by his mother and her boyfriend. I was going crazy until he was found."

"Surely his mother wouldn't have hurt him," said Lily.

"She and her boyfriend had a sale for him. They abandoned him in the alley behind Danny's. Luckily, he was found before the sale could go through." said Samuel.

"Oh no!" exclaimed Lily. "Did they get caught?"

"Yes, they are in jail. With all of the evidence against them they should get a long sentence," said Samuel.

"I'm glad you got Sam back safely," said Lily.

"Thank you," said Samuel.

"Have I distracted you enough with my horror story to get you past your visit with the magic mirror?" asked Samuel with a grin. Lily laughed and looked at Sam and Samuel.

"Yes, I guess I can drive home, now," she said.

"You can join us on the playground if you like. Sam likes to have someone to push his swing and catch him off the slide," said Samuel.

"I would like to stay for a little while. If it's okay with you Sam," said Lily smiling at Sam. Sam nodded his head vigorously. He took Lily's hand and led her toward the swings. Samuel laughed and followed.

Lily had a great time playing with Sam. Samuel mostly just stood back and watched. He stayed close by in case Sam needed him. Sam would look at him every so often, but as long as he could see his dad, he was okay. Lily finally decided she had better head for home. She hugged Sam and thanked him for showing her such a good time. She turned to Samuel and held out her hand. Samuel took her hand and gave it a squeeze. "Thank you for your understanding," said Lily.

"I'm glad you are better. Just remember, there are always children needing our love and help. Don't shut yourself off from life and love," said Samuel.

"I will remember everything you have said. You have given me a lot to think about," said Lily. She waved goodbye to her two new friends and headed for her van. The ride home was much easier than it would have been before meeting Samuel and little Sam.

Lily arrived home and carried the groceries, she had bought, into the house and put them away. She was humming softly to herself as she started to prepare supper. Doug, coming into the house to check on Lily, stopped in surprise when he heard Lily humming. He came inside and looked at her curiously. "Did everything go okay? You were gone so long I was beginning to get worried," said Doug.

Lily smiled. "Everything went fine. I stopped at Danny's for a hamburger and then I decided to go by the park for a while. It was such a lovely day," she said cheerfully.

"I'm glad you enjoyed yourself," said Doug.

"Stop worrying about me. I'm fine," said Lily patting Doug on the arm and smiling. Doug shrugged and turned to go back outside.

"I still have a few things to finish up outside. Call me when supper is ready," he said.

"Okay, agreed Lily. Doug was smiling to himself as he went outside. I should have sent her to town ages ago, he thought to himself. He was very happy to see Lily being herself again.

CHAPTER 2

Lester (Les) Hawks turned away from the mirror in his room at Hillard's Dairy Farm. He sighed. He did not know the identity of the woman in the mirror. He had heard enough stories to know the woman was probably at Danny's in town. His own boss, Jed Hillard had met Marissa through the mirror. He had never seen two people more in love. Everyone was looking forward to their wedding. It was just a few days away and Jed was rushing to try and have his house ready in time.

Les shook his head. The woman in the mirror had not looked happy to see him. He wondered if it was because he was part Native American. Maybe he wasn't what she was expecting to see. Les decided he needed to go into town and see if he could discover who the woman was. He was through with work for the day. He would just check with the boss and then he would be ready to go hunting.

Les found Jed and Marissa at the new house. They were discussing the way to furnish the living room. "Hi, Marissa. Hey, Boss, you got a minute?" asked Les.

"Sure, Les, what's up?" asked Jed.

"I was wondering if I could take off for a while. I need to make a trip to town," said Les.

"Sure, Les is something wrong?" asked Jed.

"I saw a woman in the mirror inside. The only way it could have happened is if she was looking in the mirror at Danny's. I want to go and see if I can find out who she is," said Les.

"You did not know her?" asked Marissa. "What did she look like?"

"She was small, like maybe she was underweight. She had short dark hair and the saddest eyes I have ever seen," said Les shaking his head.

"She doesn't sound familiar," said Marissa. "Good luck, I hope you find her. It sounds like she could use some love," said Marissa.

"Thanks, I'll see you all later," Les headed for his truck and departed for town.

Marissa turned and snuggled up to Jed. "Have I told you lately how glad I am you are my true love?" she whispered. Jed smiled as he kissed her. "Yes, but I always am up for hearing it again," he replied.

"I love you, soon to be Mrs. Hillard," said Jed.

"I love you, Mr. Hillard," said Marissa.

"Alright you two, is this any way to get this house built?" asked Joe, coming around the corner with his arm around Laura.

"It's the best way," said Jed with a smile.

"Laura and I thought we would come out and help, but we can make ourselves scarce if need be," teased Joe.

"Don't leave," said Marissa grabbing Laura's arm. "I need your help. I can't decide which curtains to hang in here and Jed just agrees with whatever I say. I need an honest opinion." Jed and Joe laughed as Marissa dragged Laura off to look at her curtain choices.

Jed turned to Joe to show him what he had been working on before Marissa had interrupted him to ask his opinion. He was so glad he and Joe were friends again. He had missed his brother.

Joe and Laura had been matched by the magic mirror, also. Laura had been blind at the time and Joe was attending college and working in Kansas City. The mirror had helped Laura get her sight back. She and Joe were getting to know each other and taking things slowly. Joe had started a new job with the television station. He wanted to be sure he was able to support a family before advancing their relationship.

Laura was working at the drug store. She had been off while she was blind, but the store welcomed her back when her sight was restored. Since she had got her sight back there had been an influx of customers. They were coming by to congratulate Laura and talk about the magic mirror. Laura was very patient with them. She had not known she had so many friends worrying about her.

Having friends was nice, but the highlight of Laura's day was when she and Joe finished work and spent time together. Laura tried to tell him she did not care if he was able to take care of her. She just wanted to be with him, but Joe was determined. Laura's parents were very fond of Joe and were happy he was so determined to do right by their daughter.

Les entered Danny's and went to the bar. He sat on a stool and looked around, spotting the table with the mirror, but it didn't have anyone sitting at it. He hadn't expected her to be there. He knew she had been gone for a while.

"Hi, Les, what can I get for you?" asked Lorraine the waitress.

"Hi, Lorraine, I'll just have whatever is on tap," said Les. "Were you working this afternoon?" He asked when she brought him his drink.

"Yeah, I've been here since eleven this morning, why?" she asked.

"Did you notice a young woman with dark brown hair sitting at the table with the mirror about two hours ago?" asked Les.

"Yeah, she is the only one who has sat at the table all day," said Lorraine.

"Do you know who she was?" asked Les.

"Yeah, it was Lily Hemp. Her name was Smart before she married," said Lorraine.

"She's married?" asked Les.

Lorraine shook her head. "Not anymore, her husband, her little girl and her parents were killed about three years ago when they were hit by a drunk driver." Lorraine stopped and looked hard at Les. "Wait a minute. Did Lily see you in the mirror?"

"Yes," said Les.

"I see why she was so upset. She has not got over the accident. Her brother has been doing all of their shopping. This is the first time I have seen Lily in town in ages. She wasn't ready to have the mirror show her anything," said Lorraine.

Les shook his head. This was going to be harder than he thought. "Does she live in Sharpville?" he asked.

"She lives about ten miles southwest of here. Her brother, Doug raises horses and Lily grows flowers. She sells them at the local flower shops," said Lorraine.

Les finished his drink and stood. He put his money on the counter and added a nice tip for Lorraine. "Thanks for the info," he said with a smile as he left.

Lorraine stood looking after him. She shook her head. "Why can't hunks, like him, be interested in me?" she turned and went back to work.

Les sat in his truck for a few minutes thinking about what he had just learned. He sighed and, starting the truck, headed for the dairy. Les went looking for Jed when he returned to the dairy. He found him with Joe at the unfinished house. Jed turned to him and smiled. "Well, did you find out who saw you in the mirror?" he asked.

"Yes," said Les soberly. "It was Lily Hemp."

"Lily Hemp, oh, you mean Lily Smart," said Jed. He shook his head. "You have your work cut out for you."

"What's going on?" asked Joe.

"Lily's husband, baby and parents were killed about three years ago when they were hit by a drunk driver," said Jed.

"Oh," said Joe. He looked at Les with sympathy. "Good luck."

"Thanks, according to Lorraine, she was very upset to see any face in the mirror," said Les.

"Give it time," said Jed. "Give her a chance to get used to moving on. It wouldn't hurt to pay a visit to make sure she doesn't forget about you. Her brother, Doug raises horses. Wouldn't you like to see about getting yourself a horse to ride?"

"Great idea," said Les grinning. "Thanks, Boss."

Les turned and left. He headed for the bunkhouse. He wanted to look up Doug Smart and see how soon he could go and look at his horses. Maybe, if he was lucky, he could wrangle an invite for supper. Les smiled. He was not going to let true love go unanswered. He was about to become Doug Smart's new best friend.

Les found an advertisement for Doug Smart's horses. He read through the ad and liked what he read. He wrote down the phone number and called Doug.

"Hello," said Doug.

"Hello, Mr. Smart, this is Lester Hawk. I read your ad about your horses for sale. I work for Hillard Dairy Farm, and I was thinking about finding me a mount," said Les.

"Why would you need a horse on a dairy farm, Mr. Hawk?" asked Doug.

'We use four wheelers to round up the cows for milking. I was thinking it would be much better to have a horse. I know it would be a whole lot quieter," said Les.

"It would be quieter," agreed Doug with a laugh. "Would you like to come out and look over my horses and see if you can find one to suit you?" asked Doug.

"Yes, I would like to see them. When would be a good time to come?" asked Les.

"We have about two and a half hours of daylight left if you want to come out now," said Doug.

"Thanks, I'll get there as soon as I can," said Les.

"Do you need directions?" asked Doug.

"No, I already wrote them down from your ad page," said Les.

"Good," said Doug. "I'll see you when you get here."

They both hung up and Les hurried out to his truck. He put the address into his GPS and started out for the horse farm. It was about twenty minutes later when Les pulled into the parking in front of the barn. As soon as he turned off his truck, Doug came out of the barn and came to meet him.

"Mr. Hawk," he inquired holding out his hand.

"Call me Les." agreed Les, shaking his hand.

"I'm Doug. I have some horses in the corral, if you want to take a look," said Doug leading the way to the corral. They stood for a minute, just looking over the horses. Then they opened the gate and went inside the corral to get a closer look. Les walked around, patting some on their heads, rubbing some on their flanks, and checking their mouths. He picked out three he wanted to ride and get a better feel for. He pointed them out to Doug.

They went and got a saddle and bridle. Doug helped him saddle up the first horse and opened the gate for him to ride around. Les rode him a little way trying to stay off the gravel. He turned around and headed back. When he made it back to the corral, Doug had the second horse waiting for him. He rode him around and headed back. When he arrived back Doug had the third horse waiting. Les shook his head.

"I don't need to ride him. I want this one. If he's not too expensive," said Les.

"Let's get him back inside the corral and go to my office to talk," said Doug.

"I noticed a lot of flowers. Do you sell them?" asked Les as they went inside.

"My sister grows and sells them. She also has an internet business where she sells seeds and bulbs. She ships all over the country," said Doug.

"Impressive," said Les. "The flowers look beautiful out in the field."

"Yes, they have been a lifesaver for my sister. She really needed them to focus on after the accident," said Doug.

"The accident?" asked Les.

"Yes, about three years ago a drunk driver hit the car my dad was driving. My mom, my dad, and my sister's husband and her little girl were all killed," said Doug.

"I'm sorry. It must have been a nightmare for you and your sister," said Les. "It's hard to get over a tragedy like that."

'Yes, it is," agreed Doug.

Doug showed him the papers on the horse and the price. It was about what he was expecting, so he agreed to the purchase.

"I'll need to go to the bank in the morning and switch some money from my savings to my checking. I'll come back then and pick up my new horse," said Les.

Doug agreed and they rose and started walking outside.

Lily came out the door and called to Doug.

"Supper's ready," she said before going back inside.

"Why don't you join us for supper? You can meet Lily and we can talk more. It would be nice to visit some of my neighbors again. It's been too long," said Doug.

"I don't want to be a bother," said Les. "Your sister may not be ready for a supper guest."

"Lily won't mind. She always makes plenty. Come on. I won't take no for an answer," said Doug smiling.

"Okay, I would like to stay," agreed Les.

Doug led the way inside. "Lily set another place at the table. I asked Les to stay to supper. He is buying Lord George," said Doug.

Lily brought another place setting to the table and another glass of ice for tea. "Lord George is a fine horse," said Lily.

"Yes, he is," agreed Les.

He turned so Lily got a good look at him. She gasped and turned pale.

"Are you alright?" asked Les reaching over to touch her arm. A shock went through both of them. Les drew back his hand.

"I'm sorry. I didn't mean to shock you," said Les.

"It's alright," said Lily. "I'm fine. It's just you reminded me of someone."

"Well I hope it was someone you liked," said Les with a smile.

"I don't know whether I liked him or not. I only saw him one time," said Lily.

Doug had been watching Lily and Les. He was wondering what was going on. He had not ever seen Lily so jumpy around a stranger before. She almost acted as if she knew him.

Lily finished getting things on the table while Doug showed Les where he could wash up. They were soon back and ready to sit down. Les stood behind Lily's chair waiting to help her sit. Lily was not used to having anyone help her be seated and she gave him a quick sideways look and flushed slightly. Les grinned at her and took his own seat.

Lily was quiet while they were eating. Doug and Les did most of the talking. Les was enjoying getting to know Doug and he was glad he had made Lily aware of him. He wanted her to know he was real, and he wasn't going away.

At the end of the meal, Les offered to help clean up, but Lily told him and Doug to go and finish talking. She didn't need any help.

"Thank you for supper, Ma'am, I really enjoyed it," said Les.

"It's Lily, not Ma'am, and you're welcome."

"Thank you, Lily. I'd better say goodnight. I have to be up early in the morning to milk," said Les.

He and Doug walked outside, and Doug walked over to his truck with him.

"I'll see you tomorrow," said Doug.

"I'll be here," agreed Les as they shook hands.

Les drove away very satisfied with the way things had gone. He smiled.

"Lily, my true love," he said with a grin.

CHAPTER 3

When he arrived back at the dairy, he found Jed and Joe were still in the new house. Marissa and Laura had joined them. He started to go inside the bunkhouse, but Jed called him over.

"Did you find a horse to suit you?" he asked.

"Yes, I am now the proud owner of Lord George. I have to go back in the morning after the bank opens to pick him up," said Les with a smile.

"Why do you need a horse?" asked Marissa.

"He doesn't need a horse. He wants one. He also wanted to meet Lily," said Jed, giving Marissa a hug.

"Did you meet her?" asked Laura.

"Yes, I did. I had supper with them," replied Les with a smile.

"Good work," said Jed. "How did Lily respond? Did she recognize you from the mirror?"

"Yes, she did. She tried to cover, but she knew me. I didn't let on about seeing her, but when I touched her arm, we both received a shock," said Les.

All of the other four looked at each other and smiled. They were familiar with the shock. It came with seeing your true love in the mirror.

"Why don't you invite Doug to join us for Jed's bachelor party? It's going to be in a couple of days at Danny's. The girls could call Lily and invite her to Marissa's party," said Joe.

"That's a great idea," agreed Marissa. "We need to get them both involved with our group. It will help Les if Lily gets out more."

"Alright, I'll mention it to Doug when I go to pick up Lord George. Will it be alright for me to use the small trailer?" asked Les. "I thought I would keep Lord George in the small pasture where we keep cows about to deliver, if it's okay with you?" He looked at Jed

"Sure," agreed Jed. "We only have two cows in there at this time. He will do fine there until he gets used to the place.

Les said goodnight with well wishes from the group. Laura and Marissa were especially sympathetic toward him. Jed and Joe, having gone through being seen in the mirror, knew what he was dealing with. They were all pulling for Les and Lily.

Les turned in, but he was having a hard time turning his mind off so he could sleep. Every time he closed his eyes, Lily's image popped up behind his eyelids. When he finally fell asleep, he dreamed about Lily. She was smiling at him and holding out her hand to him, but no matter how hard he tried, he could not touch her hand it was just out of his reach. Finally, Lily withdrew her hand and gave him a sad look and the dream faded.

The next morning Les remembered his dream. He wondered what it meant. His people were strong on signs. He sighed. There was no one close by he could ask. His grandmother would know but she was too far away to ask. He decided to forget it for the time being and concentrate on milking and getting to the bank when it opened.

After milking and cleaning up, Les went by the bank and transferred the money into his checking account. He had already made out the check for Doug last night. He had the horse trailer hooked to the back of his truck and, with a smile of satisfaction, he headed for the horse farm.

Doug was in the corral with Lord George when he arrived. When Les parked and went over to the fence, Lord George came over to the fence and stuck his nose out in greeting. Les rubbed his nose and gave him the sugar cube he had in his pocket.

"I think he is glad to see you," said Doug with a smile of greeting.

"I'm glad to see him, too," said Les. He rubbed the nose a couple of more times before he turned to Doug and handed him the check.

"Let's go to the office and get the ownership papers. I already have them filled out," said Doug. He came out of the corral and Les followed him to the office. On the way to the office, Les decided to bring up the bachelor party.

"A few of us guys are getting together and having a bachelor party for Jed day after tomorrow. Joe told me to see if you would like to come. We are going to have a few drinks and play some cards," said Les.

"I didn't know Joe Hillard was back in town," said Doug.

"Yeah, he is working at the television station and is engaged to Laura Sands," said Les.

"Are you sure they won't mind me being there?" asked Doug.

"They won't mind. It was Joe's idea. You would be more than welcome," said Les.

"Okay, I would like to come. What time should I be there?"

"Any time after 8:30 would be good. Danny is closing his place to everyone else, so it will be just Jed's friends there," said Les.

They went to load up Lord George so Les could be on his way. He had glanced around but had seen no sign of Lily. Lord George loaded with no problem. He acted like Les was his new best friend.

Doug Laughed. "I have never seen any horse take to someone so fast," he said.

"We are going to be great buddies, aren't we?" Les rubbed Lord George's nose one last time before shutting him in the trailer. He held out his hand to Doug. "It's a pleasure doing business with you," he said with a smile. "I'll see you at Danny's."

"The pleasure was all mine, I'll be there," said Doug as he shook

Les' hand. Les waved goodbye as he drove away. He was happy, even if he didn't get to see Lily.

⁓

Laura called Lily and invited her to Marissa's party. She was reluctant at first, but Laura talked her into it when she explained Doug would be going to Jed's party and Lily could ride into town with him. Lily finally agreed to come, and Laura gave her Marsha's address.

Marsha Dane had agreed to host the party. Tilly, Laura's sister, and her friend Macy were going to baby sit Cindy, Marsha's daughter, and Sam so Marsha could host the party. Brian, Marsha's husband, and Samuel were going to Jed's party.

Laura called Marissa and told her to pass along the news to Jed about Lily. She knew Jed would be sure and tell Les. She also called Marsha and let her know to expect an additional guest.

⁓

Doug dropped Lily off at Marsha's before heading to Danny's. He entered Danny's to the greeting of Les and Jed. Les took him around and introduced him to anyone he didn't know. Jed took him to the bar where Brian furnished him with a drink.

"So, do you want to play some cards, or do you just want to wander around, visit and listen to music?" asked Jed.

"I think I will just wander around. Maybe I'll play cards later," responded Doug.

"Sure," said Jed. "Anytime you want to play, just come on over. We are playing for quarters, so you won't be fleeced."

Doug laughed and patted Jed on the back.

"Congratulations," he said.

"Thanks," said Jed. "Marissa is one in a million. I am lucky to have met her."

"You certainly are," agreed Les.

"Yes," agreed Brian. "We are all very lucky men." The guys raised their glasses in a toast.

"Here, here," shouted someone from the card table. Jed laughed and went over to join them.

Les' phone rang, and he sat down on a bar stool and answered it. "Hello, Alex, I haven't heard from you in a while," said Les.

"Hello, Les, how have you been?" said Dr. Alex Steel.

"I'm fine, just wondering why my cousin is calling me out of the blue. Is everyone okay?" asked Les.

"We are fine. Angelica and I have a little girl. Her name is Alexandria Moon Flower," said Alex.

"Congratulations, I bet Moon Walking is happy," said Les.

"Yes, she is very pleased. She's the reason I called. She asked me to pass on a message to you," said Alex.

"Oh, what message?" asked Les.

"She said to tell you love was the answer. She also said to stop reaching so hard. Give the love time to reach for you and then your hands would meet," said Alex. "Do you know what she is talking about?"

"Yes," said Les laughing. "I was just wishing I could talk to Moon Walking. I should know she is always a step ahead. Tell her 'thanks.' I appreciate you passing along her message."

"No problem," said Alex. "Keep in touch. Family should always be there for each other. If you ever need anything, just call."

"Thanks, Alex, take care of your new treasure," said Les. They hung up and Les looked up to discover several friends had been listening to his conversation.

"I was talking to my cousin, Alex from Rolling Fork. He was passing along a message from my grandmother, Moon Walking," said Les.

"You are Moon Walking's grandson?' asked Brian. "You must have been talking to Dr. Alex Steel."

"Yes, I was. We are cousins. Alex's mother and my father were brother and sister. My mother and I moved away from Rolling Fork when my father died. She wanted to live closer to her family," said Les.

"Well, I'll be!" exclaimed Brian grinning broadly. "I can't wait to tell Marsha. We used to live in Rolling Fork. She is going to be floored."

"We moved away from there a long time ago," said Les.

"What message did Moon Walking pass on to you?" asked Brian.

"She wanted Alex to tell me love was the answer and to be patient and give love time to reach out to me then I wouldn't have to strain for our hands to meet," said Les. He laughed at the expressions on everyone's face. "Moon Walking always talks like that," he said.

"Well," said Doug. "It would be nice to know you just have to be patient to find love." Several of the men, close by, nodded their heads. Les smiled and nodded his head also. He did not want to tell anyone about Moon Walking interpreting his dream. He was glad she was providing him with an answer. All he had to do was wait. Sometimes waiting was the hardest thing to do. He hoped Lily was having a good time with the ladies. They could not go forward until Lily had coped with her past.

The other men all wandered over to watch the card game. Les and Doug were the only ones left sitting at the bar.

"I think I should give you a heads up," said Les.

"Oh, about what?" asked Doug.

"I hope you have no objections, but I am going to marry your sister," said Les.

"Lily," said Doug startled. "You just met. You hardly know her."

"I know," said Les. "Lily saw me in the magic mirror. She doesn't know I saw her, too. She is in denial and not ready for a relationship, yet, but I will be patient and give her time to get to know me. I just wanted to know if you had any objections." Doug looked at him hard for a minute. He started grinning and put out his hand.

"I have no objections," said Doug. "I just want Lily to be happy. I wish someone would see me in the mirror. It would be nice to have someone to love. Life can be lonely at times." Les shook his hand and smiled at him.

"It happened for me. It could happen for anyone. Just be ready to grab love with both hands and hold on tightly," said Les with a determined expression. Les and Doug got up and wandered over to the card table.

Lorraine came out of the kitchen. She had volunteered to fix snacks for the party. She carried a couple of large bowls, set them on the counter, turned around and went back for two more. She set one on the counter and carried one over and set it on a table next to the card game.

"Thanks, Lorraine," said Brian with a smile. "Do you need any help?"

"There are three more bowls on the counter. Two of them could be placed on tables nearby," she said.

Les and Doug headed for the counter to get the bowls. Les grabbed one and left. Doug picked up the other and glanced up into the mirror behind the counter. He stopped suddenly as he saw the reflection of Lorraine, looking back at him. His eyes flashed towards the table with the magic mirror and saw a startled Lorraine looking back at him.

Doug started smiling. Lorraine smiled back at him. Doug sat the bowl down and started walking toward Lorraine. When he reached her he held out his hand. Lorraine placed hers in it. They both pulled back at the shock.

"Hi, I'm Doug."

"Hi, I'm Lorraine."

They stood staring at each other. They were unaware of the interested audience around them. They only had eyes for each other. Les came over and slapped Doug on his shoulder, gently.

"I'll get the other bowl. Why don't you and Lorraine sit and talk?" he asked. Doug looked up at Les and then back at Lorraine.

"Okay," he said and taking her hand, he led her to a table, and they sat facing each other.

"I don't know anything about you except you are beautiful," said Doug.

"I'm Lorraine Sago. I'm divorced. I have two children, a boy, aged seven, and a girl, aged six. My ex-husband took off two years ago after cleaning out my bank account and leaving me penniless to take care of two kids. I haven't heard from him since then. I am working here to feed my kids."

"That's tough," said Doug squeezing her hand.

"I know you are probably thinking it was part his money, but it wasn't. I had the money from an insurance policy when my dad died. Charlie never worked more than a few days at a time. Most of the time, he mooched off of me. I don't know how he managed to get into my account. I didn't give him access to it. The police said they couldn't do anything because we were married. So, I borrowed some money, made sure we weren't married anymore and that I had full custody of my kids." Lorraine stopped talking and gazed at Doug. "I bet you were not expecting all of this," she said.

"I was expecting true love, just like the mirror promised. Everything else can be worked out," said Doug with a smile. He squeezed her hand.

"I was not expecting the mirror to work for me. I have looked in it every day and I never saw anyone," she said.

"It was waiting for me," said Doug with a smile.

Lorraine smiled back at him and squeezed his hand.

"I'm glad," she said.

"Me, too," agreed Doug.

Everyone in Danny's watched their progress with satisfaction. They were very fond of Lorraine. They admired her courage and determination to overcome her troubles. They did not know Doug as well, but Les vouched for him and they trusted Les. Lorraine looked up from Doug and glanced around. She flushed slightly to see everyone watching them. Doug squeezed her hand and smiled.

"It's okay. They are friends," he said.

"I know," agreed Lorraine with a smile. "They have all been very good to me since I have been on my own."

"When can I see you again and meet my future kids?" asked Doug.

Lorraine looked at him seriously. "Don't you want to take a little time so you can see what you are getting yourself into?" she asked.

"We will have all the time in the world after we get together," declared Doug. "I'm ready to get started on the rest of my life." Lorraine looked at him with tears in her eyes. "What's wrong?" asked Doug.

"I'm happy," said Lorraine. "When I was wishing the mirror would show me someone to love, I never thought I could be so lucky."

"I'm the lucky one. I have a new family and lots of love to go around," said Doug. Les came over and put his hand on Doug's shoulder. Doug looked up at him and smiled.

"Les, I would like you to meet your future sister-in-law," said Doug with a smile.

"Sister-in-law," said Lorraine.

"Yes. Les is going to marry Lily. She doesn't know it yet, so don't say anything," said Doug.

"I won't say a word," agreed Lorraine grinning at Les and Doug.

"Congratulations," said Les, shaking Doug's hand and kissing Lorraine on her cheek.

"The farm is not going to be lonely for long," said Les.

"No, it's not," agreed Doug with a smile for Lorraine.

CHAPTER 4

Lily was having an enjoyable time at Marissa's party. The ladies were all friendly and included her in their friendly talk. They played a few simple games and Marsha presented Marissa with a beautiful negligee. Marsha blushed and smiled happily at their teasing.

"I'm just glad the mirror showed me Jed," said Marissa. "I shudder to think we might never have got together."

"I know what you mean." said Laura. "It helped to bring Joe and me together and returned my sight. I will thank you forever for bringing the mirror to Sharpville, Marsha."

"How did you get the mirror?" asked Lily.

"I got it from a friend, Cindy, in Rolling Fork. She had seen her guy, who was an officer, being attacked. She called 911, and after she saw him being taken away by ambulance, she rushed to the hospital. The two had never met, only seen each other in the mirror, but they made up for lost time when she rushed into his hospital room. I worked for the police department, and I went to check on him. I heard them talking about the mirror and asked to see it. As soon as I looked into it, I was shocked to see Brian. Everyone told me Brian had been killed when his car crashed and burned, but there he was at Danny's. He didn't know me. He was hurt in the crash and had amnesia. He had wandered down the highway and been picked up by a truck driver. The truck driver dropped him off here in Sharpville. The doctors told him he could get his memory back at any time, but it had been three years and he had given up on it. When I saw him and realized he was alive, I caught the next plane to Kansas City and drove to Sharpville. He still didn't know me, but we had a connection. After a night in each other's arms, he remembered everything. I am thankful every day for Cindy loaning me the magic mirror."

Everyone had been listening in fascination as Marsha told her story. Some already knew parts of the story, but they were still fascinated.

"How did the mirror end up in Danny's?" asked Lily.

"There were three mirrors. The owner of the Gallery, where Cindy worked, had brought them back from a vacation – buying trip to Italy. She found them in a small antique store. The owner of the antique store had purchased them years before for his three daughters. He said his three daughters had found their true loves and had only sons. The mirrors only work for girls, so he said the mirrors were meant to be passed on to help others. Cindy arranged a display for one of the mirrors to be in the Gallery. She fixed another display to be shown in a museum in Denton. The daughter of the Gallery owners was managing the museum. The owner gave the other mirror to Cindy. I took it back after Brian and I decided to stay in Sharpville, but Cindy arranged the display and gave it to me. She said it was meant for the world, not just her, and she had found her true love. So, I displayed it in Danny's and Brian keeps an eye on it."

"Wow," said Lily. She looked around at everyone's faces. Everyone was just as fascinated by the story as her.

"Does it always work?" asked Lily.

"I don't know." said Marsha. "I only know it worked for me and helped Laura get her sight back."

"How did it help you get your sight back?" asked Lily.

"At first, when I sat in front of the mirror, I was blind. I had been in an accident and the doctors did not know if I would be able to see again. I couldn't see Joe, but he saw me. We talked several times through the mirror and finally over the phone. Then, when I was sitting in front of the mirror, I made a wish to be able to see Joe graduate. A white light shot out from the mirror and covered me. When the light faded, I could see," said Laura.

Lily just shook her head in amazement. "You are all so lucky," she declared.

"Yes, we are," agreed Marissa. Laura and Marsha nodded their heads. Mary, Laura's mom, reached over and gave her daughter a hug.

"We are all very lucky," said Mary. "We are thankful every day to have Marsha and Brian as friends and neighbors."

"Here, here," everyone cheered.

Marsha smiled. "Brian and I are the lucky ones. We have great friends and neighbors. We have Cindy and we will soon have a playmate for Cindy."

"You're expecting," exclaimed the ones who didn't already know. They all gathered around to congratulate Marsha.

Lily sat back and gazed at her new friends with fascination. She thought about seeing Les in the mirror. Did it mean they were meant to be together, she wondered? She shook her head. She was not as against it as she had been. Maybe it was time for her to start moving on.

She and Mark had been friends and neighbors. There was no great passion between them. They had been comfortable together and both had adored Sue. The match had been favored by her parents and Mark's parents. Mark's family had lived on the farm next to theirs. They had been friends all of their lives. When Mark died, his parents decided to move to Oregon. They wanted to be close to their daughter and their grandchildren.

They had listed their farm for sale, but it had not sold. It remained vacant. The land was just the other side of her flower fields. She had thought about buying it and expanding her fields but had decided against it. She didn't think she could handle the extra work. Lily turned as Crystal stopped beside her and smiled.

"Hi," said Crystal. "I don't know if you remember me, but we were in school together."

"Yes, I do remember you. I didn't at first. You looked familiar, but I couldn't place where I had seen you, then I heard your name and I remembered," Lily smiled at her. "It is nice to see you."

"It is nice to see you, too. I have thought about you a lot. I was so sorry to hear about your family," said Crystal.

"Thank you, what are you doing now? Are you married?" asked Lily.

"I work at Little Tots nursery, and no I am not married. I have met someone, though. I saw him, first, in the mirror. When I saw him, I did not know who he was. Then he came to town and brought his little boy by the nursery and we met. We are still working on getting to know each other. Samuel has had a lot to deal with, but we are getting closer," replied Crystal.

"Samuel is he little Sam's dad?" asked Lily.

"Yes, do you know him?" asked Crystal.

"I met him and Sam in the park. He saw I was upset. I had just seen someone in the mirror, and I was a wreck. He talked to me and then he let me play with Sam. It helped a lot," replied Lily.

"Yeah," agreed Crystal. "Samuel is a great person. Who did you see in the mirror?" asked Crystal.

"I saw Les," replied Lily. "I didn't know who he was. It wasn't Les, I just wasn't ready to see anyone, then. I sat down at the table and, when I read what the mirror said, I asked how I could find true love when my true love was gone. It answered by showing me Les. I freaked out"

"Do you think you are more ready now?" asked Crystal.

Lily smiled. "I think I just may be," she agreed.

Crystal reached over and squeezed her hand. "I'm glad," she said,

"Me. Too," agreed Lily.

Some more of the ladies joined them and the subject of the mirror was dropped. They joined in the group wishing Marissa and Jed a happy life. Lily was glad she had come. She didn't know how much she had missed having friends to visit. She had been alone with her brother for company for too long. She had also kept Doug from having a social life. He needed to get out and meet people, not stay and look after her.

"Life was for living. It was time to live," she thought.

∽

Doug was so enthralled with Lorraine he did not notice the time passing. He finally looked around and saw some of the guys leaving.

"I guess I had better go and pick up Lily," said Doug. "Will you bring the kids out to the farm tomorrow?"

"Yes, what time?" asked Lorraine.

"How about eleven? I can show you all around and then you can stay for lunch," said Doug.

"Are you sure Lily won't mind?" asked Lorraine.

"I'm sure," said Doug. "Come on, I'll walk you to your car."

Lorraine rose and walked beside him out the door. She completely forgot to tell Danny or Brian she was leaving. When they were beside Lorraine's car, she unlocked her door, then turned toward Doug. Doug pulled her close and kissed her long and deeply. When they had to breathe, he leaned his forehead against hers and sighed.

"I have been waiting to do that all night," he said.

"Me, too," agreed Lorraine.

Doug kissed her again then helped her into her car.

"I'll see you tomorrow," he said and closed her door. Lorraine smiled at him, started her car and drove out of the parking lot. Doug shook his head and headed for his truck. He had to pick up Lily. He smiled. Then he laughed. Life was good. He was so happy.

Doug went to the door of Brian and Marsha's house and knocked. Lily opened the door. She had been watching for him and had heard him arrive. She looked startled at his smiling face but turned and said goodbye to everyone and followed him to his truck. Lily kept looking at Doug curiously. Doug glanced at her and smiled.

"I met the love of my life tonight," he said. "Her name is Lorraine and she saw me in the magic mirror. She is divorced and has two children. The boy, Charles, is seven. The girl, Karen, is six. She is bringing them out to the farm tomorrow so you can meet her and the kids. I invited them for lunch."

"Okay," said Lily. "She saw you in the magic mirror in Danny's?"

"Yes, I was at the counter and I looked up and she was staring at me. I looked over at the table and she was looking up from the mirror. We talked for a long time. We are meant to be together."

"I'm happy for you," said Lily. "I will look forward to meeting them all tomorrow."

"Good," said Doug. "Just wait, you will like her."

"I'm sure I will," agreed Lily.

She was quiet the rest of the way home. She did not want to bring down Doug's mood, but she was worried he was moving too fast. She could only hope things would work out for him.

Lily sighed. She wondered what Doug would think about her seeing Les in the mirror. She wasn't ready to discuss it with him, yet. She was still trying to deal with the fact of seeing him. She wasn't ready to discuss it with anyone. Doug had been very patient with her these last three years. He deserved to have someone in his life. Maybe Lorraine would be just what he needed. He certainly seemed to think so. They would just have to wait and see.

CHAPTER 5

When Les arrived back at the dairy after leaving Danny's, he found a package waiting for him. Stu, one of the dairy workers, had signed for it and left it sitting on a table by the door. It had fragile – handle with care wrote on the box.

Les picked up the box and looked at it curiously. It said it was from Angelica Steele. He wondered what Alex's wife had sent to him.

"The best way to see what's in a package is to open it," said Dan laughing. Stu laughed and agreed with him.

Les grinned at them and opened the package. He pulled out a flower in a pot and a letter. The letter was from Moon Walking. Les read the letter and glanced at the flower, then started laughing.

"My grandmother sent it," he said. "She said the flower is called Angel Flower because of the ring of white flowers at the top. With the white petals going up the front, and the ring at the top, it looks like it has a halo.

She sent it for me to give to Lily."

"Did you tell her about Lily growing flowers?" asked Dan.

"No, I haven't talked to Moon Walking in ages. She doesn't have to be told anything. She always knows. She is a tribal elder," said Les.

"Lily is going to love the flower," said Stu.

"Yes, Moon Walking said it is a memorial for Sue, Lily's daughter," said Les. He carefully put the flower back into its box and took it to his room. He would take it to Lily tomorrow after milking was finished.

He carefully placed the box on his dresser and went to shower and prepare for bed. He couldn't stop grinning. Moon Walking had just put her seal of approval on his relationship with Lily. He could hardly wait for tomorrow.

Before he went to sleep, he closed his eyes and thought to himself, "Thank you, Moon Walking." He heard, in his mind, a distinct voice say, "You are welcome Soaring Hawk."

Les' eyes flew open and he looked around. Then he smiled. He had not been called Soaring Hawk since he had moved away from the reservation. He had forgotten about some of Moon Walking's powers.

He closed his eyes and tried to get some sleep. It took a while. His mind was very busy. He had a hard time shutting it off. He thought about Lily and prepared to dream about her. He thought maybe they could meet on the dreamscape. As he was drifting off, he caught a glimpse of Lily. She was talking to a little girl. He approached her slowly so he would not frighten the little girl off. Lily looked up at him and grinned.

"This is Sue," she said proudly.

"Hello. Sue, you are very pretty," said Les. Sue grinned shyly.

"Sue, this is Les. He is a friend of Mommy's," said Lily.

"Hi," said Sue.

"I am very happy to meet you," said Les. "I love your Mommy and I plan to take very good care of her for you. Is that okay?"

Sue stared at him for a minute, then grinned again. She nodded her head vigorously. Lily laughed and hugged Sue closely. She closed her eyes and enjoyed the feel of her little girl in her arms, again. Les put his arms around both of them and hugged them.

"Bye, Mommy," said Sue as she began to fade away.

"Bye, Baby," said Lily.

Lily turned into Les' arms and cried as he held her tightly. Les rubbed his chin on top of Lily's head and held her while she cried. Les realized Lily had stopped crying after a while and lay against him quietly. He looked down into her face and saw she was asleep, held tightly in his arms. She had her arms tight around him also. Les smiled. He eased them both down into the flowers and continued to hold Lily while she slept. Soon his eyes closed, and he slept also.

Les awoke the next morning with a smile on his face and the feel of Lily as she had been in his arms. He knew it had been a dream, but he was going to make it a reality as soon as he could.

Lily awakened and stretched. She felt better than she had in a long time. She stopped and smiled as she remembered seeing Sue in her dream and then she remembered Les being in her dream. It had felt good to know he and Sue had met, even in a dream, and liked each other. Les had held her and comforted her when she cried. It felt wonderful to be held close to him and to sleep in his arms.

She blushed, thinking about being so close to Les. It was a good thing Les didn't know what she had been dreaming. She wouldn't have been able to face him. She grinned. It was her dream, and nobody could say anything about what they did not know. Smiling cheerfully, Lily went to plan lunch for Doug's new friend and her family.

Les and his helpers finished up with the milking and taking care of the cows. Les went to take care of Lord George. He saddled him and went for a ride to make sure he was getting the exercise he needed. And then he rubbed him down and fed him. Les made sure there was plenty of water available for him and the cows in the corral. That done, he went and took a shower then headed out to deliver a special flower to a very special lady.

Les took very special care of the Angel flower. He made sure it would not be turned over or damaged in the ride to Lily's. He pulled up in front of her house and stopped. Taking the flower out of the box along with instructions on how to care for it, Les made his way to the front door.

Lily opened the door and looked in surprise. She flushed slightly. Les looked at her with surprise. He didn't know why she was flushing.

After all, she did not know she had slept in his arms in his dream. Les smiled at Lily.

"Hi," he said.

"Hi," said Lily. She glanced at the flower and her eyes widened.

"What a beautiful flower," she said. "I don't think I have ever seen one like it."

"It's called an Angel Flower. My grandmother sent it. I thought you could plant it as a memorial for Sue," said Les. Lily took the plant and held it, looking it over.

"If your Grandmother sent it, are you sure you want to give it away?" she asked.

"I'm sure," said Les. "I know nothing about growing flowers. I would probably kill it. The only safe thing to do was bring it to you."

Lily laughed.

She took the flower with her and turned toward the dining room. She had been preparing lunch. Les followed her into the dining room and watched her set the flower in the center of the table. She turned and smiled at Les.

"I don't have time to plant it now, but it will make a great center piece," she said. "I'm making lunch for Doug's friend and her children. Would you like to join us?"

"Sure, I never turn down a meal," said Les. "Can I help? I could set the table."

"Sure," agreed Lily showing him where to find dishes and utensils. "Set it for six."

Meanwhile, Doug had been having a great time showing Lorraine, Charles and Karen around. He had even arranged for Charles and Karen to have a ride on a horse. He had picked very gentle horses. He had Grant, one of his wranglers, take Charles up in front of him and he had taken Karen up in front of him. They had both loved it although Lorraine was a little nervous. They both declared they were going to learn to ride by themselves. Doug asked Lorraine if she would like a turn, but she said not this time.

Doug smiled and took her by the hand to lead the way to the house.

Karen took his other hand and smiled up at him. They all headed inside where Lily and Les were waiting for them.

"Les, it's good to see you," said Doug. "You remember Lorraine. These two are Charles and Karen."

Les came over and shook Charles' hand then leaned down and kissed Karen on the cheek. He then kissed Lorraine on the cheek and said hi. Les happened to glance over at Lily, but she quickly looked away. Les smiled. His lady did not like him kissing other ladies.

Doug pulled Lorraine closer to his side and took her over to introduce her to Lily. "Lorraine, this is my sister, Lily," said Doug. "Lily meet the love of my life."

"Hi, Lily," said Lorraine. "The table looks amazing. Your centerpiece is beautiful."

"Thank you, the flower is called Angel Flower. Les brought it to me for a memorial to Sue," said Lily smiling at Les. Les smiled back.

"Doug if you will show everyone where to wash up, we can eat," said Lily.

Doug turned and led the children to the back porch where there was a large sink and towels. Everyone could wash at once. Most of the time, when they came in from working, they came in the back door and could clean up before going on into the house. It made much less work for everyone.

They all trooped back in and took their seats around the table. They bowed their heads and held hands around the table. Doug said the blessing and then they started filling plates. Lily had made roasted chicken, mashed potatoes, green beans and carrots. She had fresh loaves of bread sliced and a strawberry cheesecake with ice cream for dessert. The kids did not complain at all, they went straight to eating. Lorraine and Doug smiled at each other as they watched them dig in.

"Did Charles and Karen enjoy meeting the horses?" asked Lily.

"They loved it. I think they have decided to have a new favorite hobby. They both declared they were learning how to ride," said Lorraine.

"I remember the first time dad put me up on a horse. I was scared to death for about a minute, then, he had to pry me loose to get me off. I loved it," said Lily.

"Yes," said Doug. "Lily was always under foot until Mom got her started growing flowers and, then, she had a new love."

"When I was on the way here today, I noticed a deserted farm next to Lily's flower fields," said Les.

"Yes, it's the Hemp place," said Doug. "They moved to Oregon after the accident. They wanted to be closer to their daughter. They have it listed for sale, but no one has been interested in it. It has been vacant for three years. There is no telling what kind of shape it is in."

"Hmmm," said Les. He looked thoughtful.

"If you would like to look at it, Marian Embers is the realtor it is listed with," said Doug.

"I just might take a look," said Les with a glance at Lily. Lily looked back at him wide eyed.

"If you really would like to look around," she said. "I can show you around. I have a key to the front door."

"Okay," said Les. "This lunch is great. I don't know when I have had such good home cooking." Lily smiled.

"It is great," said Lorraine smiling. "You can see how much my kids are enjoying it."

"I am glad everyone is enjoying everything," said lily.

"If everyone is ready for dessert, I have ice cream to go with the strawberry cheesecake," she said.

"Yeah!!" exclaimed Charles.

Everyone laughed and Doug squeezed Lorraine's hand which he was holding under the table. Les got up and followed Lily into the kitchen to help her bring in the dessert. The kids' faces lit up when they saw the large pieces of strawberry cheesecake topped with vanilla ice cream. They dug in as soon as it was put in front of them.

When everyone was finished eating, Doug took the kids and settled them in front of the television in the living room. He turned on the play station and went back to help clear the dining room.

Les, Lily, and Lorraine were clearing the table.

"Why don't you take Les over and show him the Hemp place? Lorraine and I can load the dishwasher," said Doug.

"Sure, we can," agreed Lorraine.

"Okay," said Lily. "Let me run up and get the key and we can go."

"I'll be outside," said Les.

He was pretty sure Doug was waiting to be as alone with Lorraine as he could be with two kids in the house. Les smiled and shook his head. He couldn't blame him. Being alone with Lily was something he wanted very badly. Lily came out with the key and climbed into Les' truck. He shut the door and headed for the driver's seat. He couldn't stop grinning.

Lily opened the door to the Hemp house. Les eased her back and went in first. He looked around and then stood aside so Lily could enter. Lily looked at him and smiled.

"What did you expect to see in here?" she asked.

"As long as this house has been vacant, there could have been an animal or a vagrant here," he replied seriously.

He looked at her and frowned.

"Didn't they take any furniture with them?"

"They took some. They were moving into a much smaller place out there. They told the realtor to sell it if the buyer didn't want it," said Lily.

She looked around at the furniture. It looked the worse for the passage of time.

Les started to wander toward the kitchen. Lily followed along.

"At least the cabinets are in fairly good shape," he remarked.

Les opened the back door and looked onto the back porch and into the back yard. The porch had a few squeaky boards but seemed sturdy enough. The back yard was fenced, but there was a vast amount of land beyond.

"How many acres comes with this property?" asked Les.

"There are twenty acres," replied Lily. "I thought about trying to buy it and expanding my flower fields."

"Why didn't you?" asked Les, looking at her.

"I didn't think I could handle a larger crop. I have to have help now with planting and harvesting. I didn't want to have to hire any more workers. Doug has his hands full with the horses. He doesn't have time to worry about my flower business," she replied.

Les looked at her thoughtfully for a bit, then he turned and led the way back inside to finish looking over the house. It had two bathrooms and four bedrooms. Les pulled the overhead ladder down and ventured into the attic. Lily followed closely behind him. The attic had walls and a floor in it and could be used easily. There were boxes scattered around. It needed to be cleaned out.

Les turned back and bumped into Lily, who was right behind him. He caught her arms to stop her from falling and stood holding her, looking into her eyes. Lily looked right back at him. He gradually pulled her closer until they were touching. Putting his arms around her he lowered his face and kissed her. He started off gently, then, deepened the kiss.

Lily made no objection. She kissed him back. When finally, they pulled back, Les held her close and rested his chin on her head.

"I have wanted to kiss you for a while. Holding you in my arms while you slept last night just made me want to kiss and hold you more." He whispered.

Lily looked up at him startled. "You were in my dream. You met Sue," she said.

"Yes." agreed Les. "We were on the dreamscape."

"What is a dreamscape?" asked Lily.

"It's where you go when you dream. Things can happen there when people are afraid to have them happen in real life. Like visiting Sue," Les looked at Lily and smiled.

"Will I get to see her again?" asked Lily.

"I don't know. It sounded like she told us goodbye, but anything is possible. I meant what I told Sue. I do love you and I am going to take care of you," said Les.

Lily leaned up and kissed him. Les took over and kissed her back. When they pulled apart again, they were both breathing hard.

"Do you think you could be happy living here after we fix the place up?" asked Les.

"Why here?" asked Lily.

"Because, it is close to your flower fields, we can combine them and get more helpers. When Doug and Lorraine get married, they deserve to have their privacy. We will like having our privacy, also," said Les.

"You think Doug and Lorraine will get married?" asked Lily.

"Yes, I do. He told me so last night," said Les.

'Oh," said Lily. She was silent, letting this information soak in. Les just held her close and let her think.

"Will you be able to afford to buy this place?" asked Lily.

"Yes," said Les. "I have a hefty trust fund set up by my mother's father. I haven't used it for much except buying Lord George. Will this place have bad memories for you?"

"No," said Lily. "Mark and I were childhood friends. We were in and out of each other's houses all the time. We just sort of drifted into marriage. It was what both of our families wanted."

"We are not going to drift into anything," said Les. "I am going to love you until you know no one else will do for you." He pulled her close and kissed her again.

"I already know you are my true love," agreed Lily when she could breathe again.

Les looked around. "Let's get out of here," he said. "There has got to be a better place to tell my girl I love her." Lily laughed and let him lead her down the stairs.

"I'm going to get someone to look over the place tomorrow and tell me what all needs to be done. I'm also going to talk to Mrs. Embers and see what the asking price is. Then I will make an offer." Les paused to take a breath and looked at Lily.

"You are going to marry me, aren't you," he asked.

"Yes, I think I just might,' said Lily with a laugh. Les had to kiss her again and lily was happy to be kissed.

It was quite a while before Les returned her to her house. He kissed her one last time on the porch and told her he would see her tomorrow. Lily stood on the porch and waved him off. She then went inside to spend time with Lorraine. She needed to get to know her soon-to-be sister-in-law.

CHAPTER 6

Les returned to the dairy. He saw the lights were on at Jed and Marissa's new house. He decided to go over and talk to Jed. He walked in the open front door and looked around. It was looking really good. There was a lot of work done in a short amount of time. Everyone had pitched in to help. They were all happy for Jed and wanted him and Marissa to be happy.

"Hi," said Jed coming in from another room and spotting Les.

"Hi, this is really looking great," said Les.

Jed looked around proudly. "Yes, it is. Just a few more days and I can bring my bride home," said Jed.

"I'm happy for both of you," said Les smiling at Jed. Jed glanced over at him.

"You just back from the farm?" he asked.

"Yeah, I wanted to talk to you about something," agreed Les.

"What's up?" asked Jed.

"You know the Hemp place? It's next to the farm," said Les.

"I've seen it, but I haven't been out that way in quite a while. They moved out west, didn't they?" asked Jed.

"Yeah, to Oregon, the place has been sitting empty for almost three years. It needs some work done on it, but it has possibilities. It is right next to Lily's flower fields."

"Ah," said Jed.

"I'm thinking of putting an offer in for it. I know Lily is not going to want to leave her flower fields and Doug is going to get together with Lorraine. I want to give Lily her own home," Les stopped and looked at Jed.

"Do you want me to start looking for someone to replace you," asked Jed.

"Yes, I think it would be best. One way or another, I'm going to marry Lily. It is just a question of when. I hope it won't be too long," said Les.

Jed grinned and stuck out his hand. Les smiled back and shook his hand.

"I wish you the best, you have been a great worker and I hate to lose you, but I understand. True love comes first," said Jed.

"I have loved working here, but Lily is my heart. I have to follow my heart," agreed Les.

"I understand. A short time ago I might not have, but now, I understand completely," said Jed.

"Good night, Boss," said Les as he turned and left.

"Good night, Les, good luck," answered Jed. Jed turned and went back to work. The sooner he finished, the sooner he and Marissa could move in. He did not want to wait a moment longer than he had to.

∼

The next morning after milking and taking care of Lord George, Les headed to town. He found the realtor's office and went in search of Marian Embers.

"Mrs. Embers?" asked Les.

"Yes, how may I help you?" asked Marian.

"I'm Les Hawk. I wanted to ask about the Hemp place," said Les.

Marian pulled a folder out of her files and opened it. "The Hemp place has been on the market for about three years. The price has been reduced. Are you interested in it?" asked Marian.

"The place is going to need a lot of work and I will have it inspected before I decide anything, but I am interested," said Les.

"I am sure the Hemp family will work with you on the price," said Marian. "I know they are not planning to move back here. The place has too many bad memories for them. Did you want to go out and look around?" asked Marian.

"Lily took me around yesterday. She has a key to the front door. The Hemps left it with her," said Les.

"Okay, let me give you the number for an inspector and we can get started," she wrote the number on a paper and then wrote down the asking price for the property. She also gave him a key to the place. "This price is negotiable. I'm sure we can do better. As soon as you hear from the inspector, get back to me and we can see what can be done."

"I'll be in touch," said Les. "It was nice meeting you." Les shook hands with Marian and left her office.

Marian smiled and reached for her phone. She put in a call to The Hemps. When she got Mr. Hemp on the phone. she told him about Les being interested in their place. She told him Les was seeing Lily and probably wanted it for her to expand her flower fields.

Mr. Hemp halved the price they were asking for the property. He said Lily deserved it and their son would have wanted them to help Lily. Marian hung up the phone with a big smile on her face. She rubbed her hands together. She was very satisfied. She wouldn't get as much commission, but it felt good to help friends and neighbors. She decided to wait until Les got the inspection done and then give him the news.

Meanwhile, Les had called the inspector and arranged for him to meet him at the Hemp place in a couple of hours. Les and the Inspector went over the house from top to bottom. The electricity checked out fine. The roof was okay, but the gutters were in need of cleaning and repair. There were a few boards on the porches to be replaced. Overall, the house was in better shape than he thought. After the inspector left, leaving Les a list of things to be done, the pest control man showed up. Les sat down and studied the list while the pest control man looked the house over.

When he came back to where Les was waiting, he gave Les a paper with his suggestions. Les took it and thanked him for coming. The inspection had been complimentary. While he was there, he called Lily and asked her to come over and see if there was any furniture she would like to keep.

Les was waiting inside when Lily arrived. He went over and pulled her close and kissed her as soon as she came in. Lily smiled at him.

"I thought I was here to look at furniture," she said with a smile.

"I had to think of some way to get you to myself," said Les with a grin. "Is there anything in the house you would really like to keep?"

Lily looked around.

"Isn't it going to cost us quite a bit to replace all of this?" she asked.

"No," said Les. "I have a whole house full of antique furniture stored at my grandpa's estate."

"How did you manage that?" she asked.

"My Great Aunt Hazel left it to me in her will. When I was a young, I would go over to visit Aunt Hazel. She spoiled me because she enjoyed having me around. I loved being with her. While I was there, I would help her polish and take care of her furniture. I loved it and the lemony smell. Well Aunt Hazel saw how much I loved helping and she told me she was going to leave the furniture to me when she passed. As I grew older, I forgot all about it, but she didn't. When the will was read, she had left all of her antiques to me. Her son pitched a fit. He got the house, but he thought he was going to get it all. He tried to fight the will, but her will was ironclad. My granddad moved all of the furniture to storage on his place before my cousin could do anything to stop him. We will have plenty of furniture for this place and probably some left over."

Les had been standing with his arms around Lily while he talked, and she had been looking into his eyes and smiling.

"I think we should just clean house and start fresh," said Lily. Les gave her a squeeze and led her toward the dining room. He pointed toward the large sideboard and china cabinet.

"I like this. It will fit in with my Aunt's China cabinet. Also, I wanted to ask about the boxes in the attic. I took a look at a couple of them while the inspector was here. They look like they may be things from the Hemps' family history. We need to see if they would like us to ship some or all of it to them," said Les.

"Okay,' said Lily. "We can ask about them when Marian gets in touch with them about the sale," she said.

Les nodded. "I'm ready to go ahead. This is your chance to say no if you don't want to live here."

Lily leaned closer and kissed him. "The place doesn't matter. Being together matters, I think you and I are going to do just fine here." Les pulled her close and kissed her again. He pulled back reluctantly.

"I'm going to have to go. I have milking to see to. I'll talk to Marian Embers in the morning. Dream of me," Les kissed her one more time.

Lily smiled and went out with him. They kissed again as lily entered her van to leave. Les saw her off and then headed for his truck to go to the dairy.

After milking was finished and Lord George was taken care of, Les called his mother. He wanted to tell her about Lily. He also wanted to let her know he was buying a place and he would need his furniture before long.

"Hello. Les, it's about time you called me. It has been ages," said Elaine Porter-Hawk.

"Hi, Mom, I'm sorry I have not called more often. How are you?" asked Les.

"I'm fine. Your granddad has been feeling poorly, but he will be okay in a day or so. I think he just wants attention," said Elaine.

"You and Granddad have been having this same argument ever since we moved back from the reservation," said Les with a laugh.

"How are you?" asked Elaine. "Are you ready to come back and join your granddad's company?"

"No, Mom, I told all of you I was not company material. I have met a girl. Her name is Lily. I am going to marry her as soon as I can convince her to marry me," said Les.

"Are you sure she is not after your money?" asked Elaine.

"She doesn't know I have money. I haven't told her anything about who my family is," said Les.

"I am also going to buy a farm. It's next to Lily's place where she grows flowers. As soon as I get the place fixed up, I will be sending for my furniture. It will be a while, yet. I have to fix up and paint the house," said Les.

"Do you need any help?" asked Elaine.

"No, I have it covered. If I need anything, I'll call. I just did not want you to be taken by surprise when you receive a wedding announcement," said Les.

"Lester Hawk, you had better not get married without me there," said Elaine very forcefully.

Les laughed. "I must really be in trouble if you are calling me Lester."

"I'm not joking," declared Elaine.

"I know, Mom, I promise to let you know when we make any plans. I'll try to get away long enough to bring Lily to meet you," said Les.

"If you don't, I will have to make a trip to Sharpville. I just might just make a trip down there anyway. There is a decent place to stay in town, isn't there?" asked Elaine.

"There is a nice Bed and Breakfast in town. Let me know when you want to come, and I'll get you a room. I love you, Mom. It would be great to see you," said Les.

"I'll let you know, but we'll need three rooms. My driver will need a room and you know if your granddad finds out I am on my way to visit you, he will invite himself along and if he comes, your grandmother will not be left behind." declared Elaine.

Les sighed, this was getting more complicated. "Okay, Mom, just let me know and I'll take care of it," said Les. "Bye, take care of yourself."

"Bye, Les, I love you," said Elaine.

"I love you, too," said Les as he hung up his phone with a sigh.

Les settled down to sleep. He was soon on the dreamscape. He looked around for Lily and saw her in the distance, dancing in the flowers. She was twirling around and singing to herself. Les started walking toward her. He had a smile on his face. After seeing Lily so sad, it was a pleasure to see her enjoying herself.

Les looked behind Lily and saw Sue emerging from the shadows. She was standing looking at her mother and smiling. Lily spotted her and stopped spinning. She held her arms out and Sue floated into them. Lily closed her eyes and hugged her baby close to her. Les eased closer to the two of them. Lily opened her eyes and saw him. She smiled and held out one hand to him. Les reached over and took her hand. He smiled and rubbed Sue gently on her head ith his other hand.

"Hello, Sue, I am glad you came back to visit us. It is a pleasure to see your beautiful face," said Les.

Sue giggled and gazed up at Les with a smile. Lily held her up, so she was close enough to touch Les. She reached over and touched him on his face. She giggled when his whiskers tickled her fingers. Les laughed and rubbed his whiskers on her cheek. Sue shrieked with laughter. Lily laughed also. She took one hand and felt along Les' jaw. She rubbed back over it. She loved the way it felt. Les smiled and turned his face and kissed her hand. Sue giggled again. Les tweaked her nose. Lily smiled at the them. Sue started to fade, and Lily sighed. She waited until Sue was gone and then turned into Les' arms.

"I won't cry this time," she said. "I am just so thankful I was able to see her again and I love being able to share her with you."

"Thank you for letting me meet her and get to know her," said Les. "Since she is still around, maybe we will see her again."

"Maybe we will," agreed Lily. "At least here I get to sleep in your arms. I am looking forward to having your arms around me for real."

"This is real," said Les. "It's different, but it is real. I talked to my mom about you tonight. She said she might come for a visit so she can meet you."

"Uh, Oh, what if she doesn't like me?" asked Lily.

"She will love you. Don't start borrowing trouble. I love you. I will not let anyone come between us," said Les forcefully.

Lily snuggled close and smiled. "My big strong hero," she said.

Les laughed. "Yes, I am, all yours and you are mine. Nobody is going to change that." He lay down in the flowers and pulled her towards him, kissing her gently and enjoying her closeness for a while before sleep claimed him.as

CHAPTER 7

Les called his grandfather's lawyer the next morning before going into see Marian Embers. He explained about the property and asked him to check it out and see if it was clear. The lawyer called him back two hours later and told him the property checked out. The property taxes were paid and there were no liens on it. Les thanked him and headed for the real estate office. Marian came forward to meet him when she saw him enter the office.

"Good morning, Mr. Hawk," she said with a smile and put her hand out for a handshake.

"Good morning, Mrs. Embers," said Les smiling and shaking her hand.

"I had a talk with Mr. Hemp after your visit. I told him you were interested in the property and you were also interested in expanding Lily's flower fields. He agreed to halve the asking price for the property."

Les had frowned when she started talking, but by the time she finished, he was smiling.

"He said his son would have wanted him to help Lily," explained Marian.

"We have a deal, Mrs. Embers. Write down the purchase price and I will have the bank send over a cashier's check for it," said Les.

Marian wrote down the purchase price and handed it to Les. Les took it and called the bank. He spoke to the president and explained the situation to him. Les asked him to send over a cashier's check as soon as possible. The president assured him the check would be in his hands in a short time. Les hung up the phone and turned to Marian. She had been listening to his conversation in quiet amazement. Les looked at her and grinned.

"The check is on its way. What happens next?" he asked.

"I have never had the bank jump to help anyone like this before," said Marian.

Les smiled. "My Grandfather always said to tell them what you want like it's an accomplished fact and they will do what you say because they think it's what they are supposed to do," said Les.

"Oh," said Marian. She thought about it for a minute and then shook her head to clear her thoughts. "As soon as we get your check we go into escrow until we check out taxes and title."

"The taxes are paid up and the title is clear," said Les. "I had my Lawyer check it out."

"Who is your lawyer?" asked Marian.

"Mason Folston," replied Les.

"Do you want me to send copies of the sale and deed to his office for him to check?" asked Marian.

"As soon as the check gets here, and we sign everything, you can fax copies to Mason and he will okay them," replied Les.

"You don't waste any time when you make up your mind," remarked Marian.

Les smiled at her. "I found some boxes in the attic of the Hemp place. They look like they may have some historical things about their family. When you talk to them would you ask them if they would like for us to ship the boxes out to them?" Marian made a note of his question. "Also, about the furniture, the only thing in the house we would like to keep is the sideboard and china cabinet in the dining room. Everything else can be cleared out and sold. You can send the money from the sale to the Hemps."

"Okay, I'll get it cleared out as fast as I can," agreed Marian.

There was a knock at her door and a bank employee entered and had Les sign for a cashier's check. Les signed and passed the check to Marian after a quick glance to be sure it was in order.

Marian looked at the check and pushed the sale papers across her desk for Les to sign. When he had signed, she took the papers and faxed them to Mason Folston. Marian shook her head. Mason Folston was one of the top attorneys in the state. Marian glanced at Les while they waited for an answer to the fax. Just who was this man who wandered into her office paid cash for a place, told the bank what to do, and had this famous lawyer on call? She didn't have any answers, but she sure was curious. The fax machine dinged and spewed forth papers. Marian took the papers and after looking at them, she handed them to Les.

Les looked them over and grinned. "Everything is fine," he said.

"You have yourself a property, Mr. Hawk," said Marian.

Les put his hand out for a shake and smiled as Marian shook it. "It was a pleasure doing business with you, Mrs. Embers."

"The pleasure was all mine, Mr. Hawk," replied Marian.

Les left the real estate office with a satisfied grin on his face. He dropped by a local construction company and made arrangements for them to do all the repair work on the house He also contracted for them to build a stable for Lord George. He told them he would have more work for them to do after he had finished the house and had a chance to look around.

Les called Lily; but did not get an answer. He thought she was probably in the flower fields, so he decided to try again later. He was so excited to be a property owner, he could hardly stand not telling someone, but he did not want to say anything to anyone before talking to Lily. If she heard about it from someone else, she may be upset. He thought about it for a minute, then jumped in his truck and headed for the farm.

When Les pulled to a stop at the farm, he saw Lily taking a basket of flowers into her flower workshop Les quickly exited his truck and headed her way. He stopped just inside the door and looked around. Everything was very well organized. There was cool storage for the flowers. A long table was in the center of the room. Lily was at the table working with the flowers, she had just brought in.

"Hi," said Les as he made his way toward her.

Lily looked up and smiled. She quickly lay down the tools she was working with and turned to greet him. Les walked right up and put his arms around her. He pulled her close and laid his lips on hers. Lily snuggled closer, so Les deepened the kiss. When he drew back, he smiled at her.

"It's very nice sleeping in your arms," said Lily smiling up at him. "I haven't had such restful nights in years."

Les grinned. "I loved holding you while you slept. You had better enjoy the restfulness. When we are married, I don't think our nights are going to be so restful. Nice, but not restful," Lily just smiled and snuggled closer to him.

"I came out to tell you about our new place," said Les. "Everything is settled, and we now own the place next door. Marian is going to have the furniture moved out and see if the Hemps want the boxes in the attic. I have contractors coming out this afternoon to start repairs and build a stable for Lord George."

'You have been busy," said Lily. "I thought it would take longer for everything to be settled."

"Sometimes it does. The Hemps came down on the price because Marian told them it was for you. I decided not to haggle and accepted the price." Les shrugged his shoulders. "I paid for the property, so we didn't have to wait for a mortgage to be checked out. I had my lawyer look it over and he assured me everything was in order. So, now we are on our way to beginning our life together." Les hugged her close again and kissed her.

"When will we be able to move in?" asked Lily smiling up at Les.

"Maybe, a couple of weeks, we will see how fast I can get people moving. As soon as the furniture is cleared out, we will have to go through and see what colors you want everything painted. I will send for my furniture and what we don't use can be stored in the attic."

Les pulled back and looked around. "Do we need to build you a workshop like this at our new home?" he asked.

Lily looked startled. "I hadn't even thought about it," she said. She thought about it for a minute, then, she shook her head. "We can do it later. I can still use this building until we get settled into our new home and can afford to build some more."

"We can afford to build whatever you want," said Les. "I have the money. I told you I have a trust fund."

"I want to contribute, too," said Lily. I earn pretty well from my internet business. I haven't been spending much since the accident. I want this to be both of us working together."

Les looked at her earnest expression and then smiled. "We will work it out. Maybe you can decorate our nursery," he said. "I do hope you are ready to start a nursery. I know you are a great mother and Sue would be happy to see you happy."

Lily sighed and laid her head on Les' chest. "I am so ready to start a nursery with you. I can just see you walking around with a little dark-haired boy at your side, determined to keep up with his daddy."

Les smiled and hugged her. "Maybe two or three, and a couple of little blond-haired girls to keep them in line."

Lily laughed. "We had better get busy," she said looking up at him with a smile. "It sounds like you have plenty of work planned for me."

"I'll be right there with you, all the way," assured Les as he kissed her again. Les sighed and pulled back. "I have to go and help with the milking. I've already told Jed to start looking for someone else, but I doubt he has anyone, yet. I just had to tell you about our home, and I couldn't get you on your phone."

"I left it on the charger," said Lily.

"I don't mind. This was much nicer than a phone call," said Les kissing her again. "Yes. it was," agreed Lily.

Lily walked him out to his truck and waved goodbye as he drove away. When she turned, she saw Doug walking toward her from the barn.

"Was Les just leaving?" he asked.

"Yes, he came by to let me know he bought the Hemp place," said Lily.

Doug looked startled. "He moves fast," Doug said smiling.

"Yes," agreed Lily smiling back. "He asked me to marry him and I said yes."

Doug hugged her. "I just want you to be happy. If Les makes you happy, I'm all for it." Lily accepted his hug and smiled. She was very happy. Lily pulled back and smiled at Doug.

"I had better finish up with the flowers so I can start supper. When are Lorraine and the kids coming back?" she asked, walking toward her workshop.

"I'm going into town to see them tonight, so I won't be here for supper," said Doug looking sheepish.

Lily laughed. "It's okay I'll just call Les and invite him to come back after milking. It's okay," she said, patting his arm.

Doug gave her a quick hug and headed back to the barn. Lily turned toward the house to get her phone off the charger so she could call Les. She stood at the counter and called before going back outside.

"Hello," said Les.

"Hi," said Lily. "How would you like to come to supper after milking?" she asked. "Doug is going into town and it's no fun cooking for one."

"I'll be there. I can promise you won't be bored," laughed Les.

"See you then," said Lily with a smile.

Les hung up the phone with a satisfied sigh. He hurried on toward the dairy. The faster he was done, the faster he could get back to Lily.

As soon as milking was over, Les was in his truck on his way to Lily. When he was about to turn into the road to Smart farm, he saw a man walking down the road toward him. The man looked like he was in a daze and he had a baby, wrapped in a blanket, in his arms. Les stopped the truck and waited for him to get closer. When he could see the man's face, he saw his face was wet with tears.

Les got out and approached the man. "Hello, can I help you?" he asked. The man looked at him blankly for a minute. Then he looked down at the baby.

"I need to get to town. My car wouldn't start," he said.

"Is this your baby?" asked Les.

"No, it's my sister's baby. She died in childbirth. I just got back, but I was too late. She was already gone. I need to report it to someone."

The man looked so dazed. Les didn't think he knew what he was doing. Les led him over to his truck and help him into the passenger side. He then turned onto the road toward the farm. They could call for help from the farm, and it would get there faster. When they were at the farm, Les went around and helped the man out and led him toward the door.

Lily opened the door and started to smile. She looked at the man and her smile faded.

"Greg," she said. She looked at the baby in his arms and reached for it. She opened the blanket and looked at the baby. "This is a newborn," she gasped. "Where's the mother?"

Greg had tears running down his face again. "Erin didn't make it. When I got home, she was barely hanging on. As soon as she gave me the baby, she drew her last breath." He was crying openly now.

"Who is he?" asked Les.

"Their farm is the other side of the Hemp place. Greg has been gone for over a year. He was working in Kansas City and sending money home for Erin. Their parents were gone it was just the two of them. Erin had a boyfriend, but he wasn't worth much. It looks like he left Erin and took off. I didn't know she was expecting. I haven't been getting out much. I should have checked on her," said Lily.

Les put his arm around her. "This is not your fault. I am sure there are a lot of people to blame, but you are not one of them. We need to call the sheriff and get someone out there. Can you take care of the baby?"

"Yes, I still have all of Sue's baby stuff. I'll dig out a couple of bottles and see if I can get a little milk down him. I think I have a small bit of goat milk. Cow's milk is not good for a new-born." Lily went to look for a bottle and Les pulled out his phone to call the sheriff. Greg was sitting in a chair with his head hanging down crying.

"The sheriff is sending someone out," said Les as Lily came back in with the baby. She was feeding him a bottle.

"Good," said Lily. I didn't fix much. He won't take much to start."

Lily went over and sat down beside Greg. "What happened to Erin's boyfriend, Greg?" asked Lily. "I didn't know she was expecting."

"I didn't know either," said Greg. "Erin's boyfriend was killed a couple of months ago in a bar fight. He was running around on her. I was working in Kansas City and I got laid off when work slowed down. I got a letter from Erin and she told me he was gone, so I decided to come home and check on her. My car died on me a little way from the house. When I walked in, I heard Erin moaning. She was covered in blood and was holding tight to this little fellow. She handed him to me and died. I didn't know what to do. I covered her with a blanket and started walking."

"You did just as you should. We'll help with the baby and Les has called the sheriff. This gentleman here is Les Hawk, my fiancé. Les, this is Greg Daleen. He and his sister Erin have been our neighbors forever," said Lily.

Greg glanced up at Les. "Thanks for helping me," he said.

"You're welcome." said Les.

There was a knock at the door. When Les opened the door, a sheriff's deputy was there.

"Are you the ones, who called about a dead body?" he asked.

Greg moaned and Les pulled the deputy onto the porch.

"The deceased is his sister. He returned to find her dead from childbirth. He just got back from Kansas City and did not know she was expecting. I picked him up on the road. His car had died, and he was walking to town carrying the baby. They live the other side of my property. I own the hemp place. Their name is Daleen," Les waited for the deputy to say something.

"I know where the place is. I'll check it out. Does the baby need to be taken to the hospital?" he asked.

"No, Lily is taking care of him. If we have any problem with him, we will take him in," said Les.

"Okay, I'll be back after I check on Erin," said the deputy.

"You know Erin," said Les.

"We went to school together," said the deputy shaking his head. He went to his car and left. Les turned and went back inside.

CHAPTER 8

When Doug arrived home and saw the deputy sheriff's car out front, he hurried inside to see what was wrong. He looked around and spotted Greg, sitting in a chair, with the deputy sitting next to him. Les was sitting on the couch with his arm around Lily. Lily had a cradle next to her with a baby in it. Doug took all of this in quickly as he stood in the door.

"What's happened?" he asked. "Greg, I didn't know you were back. Where's Erin?" Greg just hung his head.

Lily got up and went to Doug. "Erin is gone," she said hugging Doug.

"Gone," he repeated. "How?"

The deputy turned and looked at Doug. "The doctor said she hemorrhaged after giving birth. She managed to take care of the baby, then she started bleeding and had no way to get help."

"Baby? I didn't know she was expecting. Why didn't she call us?" asked Doug.

"Because the scum she was living with was drinking up all of the money I sent her, and she couldn't pay the bills. The phone was cut off. There was a notice on the front door when I arrived about the electricity being cut off. I don't know what happened to her car. It wasn't there. He must have taken it, too." Greg was furious. Mostly with himself because he hadn't been there when his sister needed him.

Doug went over and put a hand on Greg's shoulder. "I'm sorry, Greg. I can't believe she's gone."

The deputy got up and turned to leave. "Erin has been taken to town. They will take her to the funeral home. You can get in touch with them about the arrangements. The DCPS (department of Child Protective Services) will probably be in touch about the baby." he said.

"Why would the DCPS be in touch about the baby?" asked Lily.

"Because both his mother and father are gone. They will have to decide custody," said the deputy.

"They are not taking him," declared Lily.

Les came over and put an arm around her. "Calm down, we won't let anything happen to him." he promised.

Lily turned into his arms and hugged him tightly.

Doug went out with the deputy and talked with him outside before he left. Lily turned and looked at Greg. He still looked dazed.

"Greg have you had anything to eat?" she asked.

Greg shook his head. "I couldn't eat anything, Lily. I could use something to drink," he said.

"I'll get you something," said Doug coming in the door and heading for the drinks.

"Greg, I'll fix you a room. You are not going back to your house tonight," said Lily.

"I don't want to be a bother," objected Greg.

"It's no bother. I'll get it ready." She took Les' hand and led him along with her as she left the room to fix a bed for Greg.

Lily turned and with her arms around him looked into Les' eyes. "Can you stay, too?" she asked.

Les kissed her gently. "Just let me call Jed and let him know I won't be there in the morning and make sure Lord George is taken care of. I won't leave your side. I can help with the baby."

"Do you think we can stop the DCPS from taking the baby?" she asked.

"I'll call my lawyer first thing in the morning and he can take care of it. They won't take the baby," Les declared firmly.

Lily gave him another hug and went to fix a room for Greg. Les turned and went back into the living room. Greg and Doug were talking quietly so they would not wake up the baby.

"I don't know how to take care of a baby. How am I supposed to look for work with a baby to take care of?" worried Greg.

Les sat back on the sofa. "What type of work are you looking for?" he asked.

"I have been working as a helper on a construction job. The work slowed down, and I was laid off. I haven't saved any money. I was sending most of my check to Erin to help her. The property taxes will be overdue. I'll probably lose the place," Greg sighed.

"All of this can be taken care of in the morning. You need to try and get some rest. We can help you deal with everything tomorrow," said Doug.

"Don't worry about the baby," said Les. "Lily and I will take him. You will still be living next door and be his Uncle Greg. We can make a good home for him and Lily will take very good care of him. It will also keep the DCPS from getting involved."

Greg looked at him. "Do you think Lily will want to keep him?" he asked hopefully.

Les grinned. "I think you would have to pry him out of her arms to take him away from her."

Greg looked relieved. "I would love for him to be in Lily's care. I think Erin would have liked to know he was with Lily."

Lily came back into the room. "Your room is ready whenever you want to lie down, Greg. It is the third door on the left. The bathroom is the next door down."

"Thanks, Lily. Les said you and he would like to take the baby and raise him."

Lily looked at Les and smiled. "We would love to take him, Greg. You can be sure he would be safe and happy with us," she said.

"Okay," said Greg. "I think Erin would have approved. I think I'll lie down for a while. Thank you all for all of your help. I'll see you in the morning." Greg headed up to his room. He knew he wouldn't sleep, but he just wanted to be alone to mourn his sister. Doug and Lily understood. They had gone through their own times and they knew sometimes you just wanted to be alone.

Lily came over and sat on the sofa beside Les. "Thank you," she said as she leaned in and kissed him. "You know we never did eat our supper. Are you hungry?"

"I could eat," said Les with a grin.

"Doug, you want to join us for supper?" asked Lily.

"I ate earlier, but I wouldn't mind some dessert," said Doug.

"How do you know I have dessert?" asked lily. They rose and headed for the dining room. Les picked up the cradle and took it along with them. Lily grinned at him.

"You always have dessert," said Doug. Lily just smiled and began to set the table. Les placed the cradle to the side where the light would not shine on it before joining Lily. Doug went over and stared down at the baby.

When Lily and Les brought the food and plates to the table, Doug turned with a grin when he saw the large slice of cake.

"He's a cute little fellow," said Doug. "What are you going to call him?"

"He's going to be Eric Lucky Hawk," said Lily. "The Eric is after Erin and we will call him Lucky because we are lucky to have him."

Les squeezed her hand and smiled. "Moon Walking said to give Lucky a kiss from her. She said he will grow up to be a great warrior."

"When did she tell you this?" asked Doug.

"Last night," said Les. He gave a really big smile.

"You didn't even know about him last night," objected Doug.

"Moon Walking is always one step ahead. I didn't know what she was talking about when she said it, but now it all makes sense."

Lily burst out laughing. "You are going to have to take me to meet Moon Walking. I am going to love having her for a grandmother," she said.

"She would like to meet you and little Lucky. We can go to meet her on our honeymoon," said Les. "I should warn you; she calls me Soaring Hawk."

"I love it. I just might start calling you Soaring Hawk," said Lily.

"Okay, just not in front of my mother and grandfather. He doesn't like to be reminded about my Indian blood," said Les.

"Why not?' asked Doug.

Les shrugged. "He's very proud of the Porter heritage. He doesn't like to think about the Indian side. What he doesn't take into consideration is the Indian side has a greater heritage than the Porter side."

"Wait a minute," said Doug. "Is your grandfather Jacob Porter, the software king?"

"Yes," said Les. "He wanted me to go into the business, but I just wasn't cut out to stay inside all day."

"I bet it didn't go down very well with him," said Doug with a grin.

"He has gotten used to it and I think he respects me for standing up to him," said Les.

Lily had been listening to their conversation with a puzzled expression on her face. Les squeezed her hand.

"Don't worry about it. He's just my grandfather. He will probably spoil our kids rotten and try to talk them into joining his company when they grow up," he said with a laugh.

Doug shook his head and got up to take his plate to the kitchen. He put it into the dishwasher and said goodnight on his way back through.

Les and Lily cleaned the table and put their dishes in the dishwasher. Lily turned the dishwasher on, and they headed upstairs with Les carrying the cradle. Lily had pre-fixed some bottles and left them in the refrigerator for later use.

Lily led the way to her room and they set the cradle to the side so it would not be in the light, but it was close enough to reach in a hurry.

Lily turned to Les and went into his arms. He held her close and kissed her.

"I just want to hold you close in a bed instead of the flowers," said Les. "I have enjoyed you sleeping in my arms on the dreamscape, but I am sure we both will enjoy it more when we can wake in others arms also."

"Anything bringing us close, I'm all for," said Lily with a smile. "I don't know what I did to deserve you in my life, but I am very thankful you are here and loving me."

After another kiss, Lily pulled back. I have a bathroom through the door over there," she said, pointing. "You want to go first while I round up some clothes and baby diapers for Lucky?"

Les headed for the bathroom and a had quick shower while Lily gathered what she needed for the baby and clothes to sleep in. When Les came out, he had a towel wrapped around his waist and Lily smiled as she passed him on the way to take her turn in the shower.

Les turned out all of the lights except a lamp. He left it on so they could see the baby. He dropped his towel on a chair and crawled into bed. He pulled the covers up to his waist and waited for Lily to come out of the bathroom.

When Lily came out, Les smiled at the long gown she was wearing.

"I just want to hold you in my arms," he said holding the covers back for her to get into the bed. When she settled, he pulled her close and gave her a quick kiss. "Good night," he whispered.

It took a little while, but they both fell asleep, only to awaken three hours later to a small cry from Lucky. They both climbed out of the bed and Les reached Lucky first. He started bouncing and soothing him.

"Why don't you go and get his bottle while I change him," said Les.

"Do you know how to change him?" asked Lily.

"Of course, I lived on a reservation until I was eleven. We all pitched in and helped with the little ones," said Les.

"Okay, I'll be right back," promised Lily.

Les laid Lucky on the bed and, taking the diaper Lily had left close by, he quickly removed the old diaper and put the new one in place. He powdered the tiny bottom and fastened the new diaper. He picked up Lucky and started bouncing him again. He talked to him all the while and Lucky had quit fussing and watched him like he knew exactly what he was saying. Lily smiled when she came in the door and saw them. She came over and took Lucky to feed him.

"I knew you would be an amazing dad," she said. Les leaned down and kissed her neck. He looked down at Lucky and found his little eyes open and staring right at him. Les smiled at him. "Enjoy your bottle little one. Dad's going to enjoy your mom." Lucky closed his eyes and continued to drink. Les laughed softly. Lily grinned up at him. She finished feeding Lucky, burped him and settled him back in his cradle. Then they settled down for a couple more hours of sleep.

The next morning, while lily was taking care of Lucky, Les went into the living room to call Jed. He had texted him the night before to let him know he wouldn't be there, but he wanted to fill him in and let him know what was going on.

"Hello," said Jed.

"I hope I didn't wake you," said Les.

"No, I was awake. I was going to help out in the barn," said Jed. "What's going on?" Les filled him in on everything and then told him he wouldn't be able to help for a few days and asked for Lord George to be taken care of.

"Of course, we will take care of your horse," said Jed. "Don't worry. Do what you have to do to help and let me know if there is anything we can do to help. Tell Greg we are all sorry and let us know about the funeral."

"Okay, Boss, I'll tell him," Les hung up and called his lawyer. He explained the situation to him and asked him to arrange for him and Lily to have immediate custody of Lucky. The lawyer assured him he would take care of it and would be back in touch later in the day. Les hung up the phone with a sigh of satisfaction and went to find Lily.

Lily had taken care of the baby and had him sleeping while she fixed breakfast. Les set about helping her and they soon had a meal on the table. He told her about talking to his lawyer and they would hear from him later in the day. They had just sat down when Doug and Greg entered the dining room. Lily insisted Greg sit down and try to eat something before they went to town.

After they had all, including Greg, finished eating, Doug called to find out which funeral home Erin had been taken to. Lily stayed home with Lucky while Les, Doug, and Greg went to the funeral home to see about the arrangements.

The funeral director met them at the door. Greg started asking about paying it off in installments. Les handed the director his credit card and told him to take everything out of it. Greg turned to him in astonishment.

"I don't know when I'll be able to pay you back," he said in embarrassment.

"I am not doing it for you. I am doing it for Lucky. I would not be able to look my son in the eye if I did not give his birth mother a proper send off. If you still want to work for me, I will have lots of work to do on my place. I'm sure you'll soon have everything, at your place, worked out," said Les. He didn't want to embarrass Greg by just paying for the funeral. After all he was Lucky's uncle.

"Thank you," said Greg. "I appreciate all of you helping. I want my sister to have a good send off, also. I just didn't know how I was going to accomplish it." Les placed his hand on Greg's shoulder.

"Anything you need, just ask. You are family. In our tribe, families take care of each other," said Les.

"I think I will like being a part of your family," said Greg.

They went around and picked out everything and soon had the funeral set for the next day. When they left the funeral home, Les texted Jed and gave him the information and asked him to spread the word. He asked him to see if the pastor at Marissa's church would say a few words.

Jed texted him back a short time later and said everything was a go. Doug and Les took Greg by Danny's and got him some coffee. Lorraine was working and she came over and kissed Doug and said hello to Greg,

"I was sorry to hear about Erin. When is the funeral?" asked Lorraine.

"Tomorrow at two," said Doug.

She turned around and called out to Danny. "I won't be here tomorrow. I have to go to my friend's funeral," she said.

"We will be closed tomorrow from twelve, so we can all go to the funeral," said Danny. He came forward and shook Greg's hand. "I'm sorry about Erin," he said.

"Thank you," said Greg.

They stayed a few more minutes and then headed back to the farm. They went inside to find Lily in the living room feeding Lucky a bottle.

Les went over and sat down beside her and smiled at Lucky. Lucky grinned back at him. "Did you see him? He smiled at me," said Les. Lily looked at Lucky and then at Les. "It was probably just gas," said Lily. Les shook his head. "He smiled." He insisted.

His phone rang and he went into the dining room to answer it. When he came back a few minutes later, he was smiling.

My lawyer just called. He talked to a local judge and arranged everything with him for Lily and me to have custody of Lucky. He had the judge call DCPS and tell them not to pick him up. We have to appear before the judge in two hours with Greg and sign the papers.

"You are naming the baby Lucky," said Greg.

"Yes, we are naming him Eric Lucky Hawk. Eric is after Erin. Lucky is because we are Lucky to have him. I hope you don't mind we didn't ask you first," said Lily.

Greg was shaking his head, "Erin would have liked the name. She would be proud to have him called lucky. Well, what are we waiting for? Let's head to town".

They gathered everything for the baby. Lily pulled out an old diaper bag and filled it. "We need to pick up some formula while we are in town. We are getting low on goat's milk," said Lily.

They piled into Lily's van because it had more room. Lily sat in the back seat. She had an old car seat of Sue's for the baby. Les sat in back with her and Greg sat in front with Doug who was driving.

When they arrived at the courthouse, the clerk took them straight back to the judge's chambers. The judge came around and shook their hands. He paused at Les. "Mr. Hawk, it is a pleasure to meet the grandson of Jacob Porter. I have long been an admirer of his. Mr. Folston explained the situation to me, and I have the papers he faxed to me for your signatures. This custody is temporary. If no one changes their minds in six months, it will become a permanent adoption. Do all of you understand this?"

He looked around and everyone nodded, including Greg. The judge nodded in satisfaction and had them sit down and start signing papers. When they finished and left the judge's chambers, Lily leaned against Les.

"Thank goodness it's done. I had no idea there was so many papers to be signed for a simple custody agreement," she said.

Les hugged her and grinned down at her. "Let's go to the store for formula," he said. Lily and Les headed for the grocery store. Greg and Doug decided to wait in the van. Greg was not up to meeting anyone else for now.

While they were in the store there were several people who stopped them and asked about Erin and the funeral. All of the women made a fuss over Lucky. Les and Lily were very patient with them, but they were glad Greg and Doug had waited in the Van. They made their purchases as fast as they could and left the store.

CHAPTER 9

The next day the funeral home chapel was packed with friends and neighbors attending Erin's funeral. Greg was looking around in amazement at the large crowd. Lily took his arm and guided him to a seat in front. Les was beside her, carrying Lucky. Doug had spotted Lorraine and went to bring her up to sit with them.

At 2 o'clock the pastor from Marissa's church came forward and introduced himself and went to the front to talk. Marissa had filled him in on Erin, so he had some nice things to say about her. He reminded everyone that Erin would live on in Lucky.

After the pastor sat down, there was a line of people coming forward to speak. They mainly said they would miss her, and she was a good person.

Some ladies came forward to sing. They sang How Great Thou Art and I'll Fly Away. Then Marissa, Laura, and Tilly came forward and sang The Old Rugged Cross. When they sat down, Lily looked over at Greg and saw he was silently crying. She took out some tissues and handed them to him. He took them silently and wiped his eyes.

They all rose when the service ended and started to leave. A lot of people came by and shook Greg's hand and expressed their sorrow.

When they were out of the chapel, they got into their van to follow the hearse to the cemetery. Erin was being buried in the Smart family cemetery. It was a private cemetery out at their farm. A few people followed them out, but it was not a large crowd. Jed and Marissa, along with Sara, Jed and Joe's mother had come. Joe and Laura also followed. Lorraine was behind them in Lily's van.

When they left the burial and headed for the house, they found food had been brought in by the town's ladies. There was quite a crowd waiting for them. Lily looked over at Greg and frowned. She then looked at Les. Les squeezed her hand.

"They are just trying to help the only way they know how," he said.

"I know," agreed Lily. She shrugged her shoulders. There was nothing she could do about it. She remembered when Sue died. She had not wanted to deal with all of the people. She had left Doug to deal with them. She really owed him a big thank you, for shielding her back then. Maybe she could help get Greg out of the line of fire as soon as possible.

Jed and Marissa had to leave because Jed had to see about the milking. Sara went along with them. Soon after they left, Joe and Laura followed them. Lorraine took Lucky upstairs to feed him and let him sleep away from the crowd.

Lily waited until most people had spoken to Greg, then she asked Doug to take him out to help with the horses. Doug excused himself and Greg and they headed out to the barn.

Les and Lily were left dealing with their well-intentioned neighbors. Thankfully, they started leaving a few at a time. Finally, only one couple was left. They looked like they had been waiting for the others to leave.

They were Mr. and Mrs. Stoddard. They lived on the other side of Greg's place. Lily looked at them curiously. She couldn't imagine why they were waiting. Mrs. Stoddard looked like she was about to cry. Mr. Stoddard cleared his throat to speak.

'Is something wrong?" asked Lily.

"We just wanted to say we were sorry about Erin. Greg had asked us to keep an eye on her. We did for a while, but her friend threatened us with a gun. He told us he would shoot us if we came back. We reported it to the sheriff, but he told us he couldn't do anything because the guy lived there. He had a right to make us leave. We would have told Greg, but we didn't know how to get in touch with him. Then my wife became ill and we were in and out of the hospital a lot and we did not know he had died." He paused and his wife gave a sob.

Lily came over and sat beside her and hugged her. Les laid his hand on Mr. Stoddard's shoulder. "This is not your fault," said Les. "It was just an unfortunate set of circumstances. Nobody could have known what was going to happen. Erin could have come to Lily when she found out she was expecting. Even if she had to walk, it's not so far, but she didn't. She thought she could handle things, and she did. She delivered the baby and took care of him. She had no idea she would start bleeding. She did the best she could. All any of us can only do our best. Some things are just meant to be. Erin's at peace now. Don't worry, I'll tell Greg what happened."

"Are you all right, now?" Lily asked Mrs. Stoddard.

"No, I have cancer. I have to go back for treatments," answered Mrs. Stoddard.

"I'm sorry," said Lily hugging her again. "If there is anything we can do to help, let us know."

"Thank you," said Mr. Stoddard as they rose to leave.

Les and Lily walked them out and said goodbye again. They came inside and collapsed on the sofa. Les put his arm around Lily and held her close.

"I'm glad it's over," said lily.

"Me too," agreed Les. "It doesn't make for a happy time for Jed and Marissa's wedding in a few days.

"Oh, my goodness," exclaimed Lily. "I had forgotten about it. I hope this doesn't put a damper on their day."

"Maybe it's just what everyone needs to know that life goes on," said Les.

"You may be right," agreed Lily.

Les pulled out his phone. He called the people he had cleaning out his house. He told them to go over to Greg's place and clean out Erin's room. He told them to take the bed out and burn it. When he hung up his phone, Lily leaned over and kissed him. "I am glad you did that," she said. "Greg did not need to deal with it."

"I hope he won't be mad I did not ask him first," said Les with a frown. "He's just going to get used to me. I tend to do things and ask questions later."

Lily laughed. "I've noticed," she teased.

Les grinned at her. "We have to get into the jewelers and see about getting you an engagement ring. I want you to pick something you like enough to wear for the next fifty or sixty years."

Lily laughed. "Is that all?" she asked. "I was figuring on a lot longer for us to be together."

Les pulled her close and kissed her. "I was thinking fifty or sixty would make a good start." He leaned over for another kiss. Lily kissed him back with enthusiasm.

"Okay you two, break it up," said Doug coming into the room with Greg. "What's to eat? I'm starved."

"There is a whole kitchen of food and you're starved," said Lily.

"Well, a guy has to eat," laughed Doug heading for the kitchen. Greg came over and sat in a chair. He looked like he wanted to say something; but did not know where to start.

Les and Lily waited patiently for him to speak.

"I don't know how I will ever be able to thank you all for everything you have done for me and for Erin. I don't know what shape the farm is in, but I'm not good at farming. I went away looking for work in the first place because I was not doing any good on the farm, but it is not easy to find work in my field with my limited education. The only thing I could find was construction and I wasn't very good at it. When the lay-offs started, I was the first to go." Greg paused to think.

"What field of work were you interested in?" asked Les.

"I wanted to work on computers, maybe writing programs. I did really well on them in high school, but I couldn't afford to go on to college. The companies all require at least some college before hiring."

"Did you try Porter Industries?" asked Les.

"Yeah, I applied to them online. I never heard back from them," said Greg.

Les turned to Lily. "Do you have a laptop?" he asked.

"Sure, it's in my office. I'll get it." she got up and headed for her office. She was back in just a few minutes with her laptop. She handed it to Les. He set it on the coffee table and turned it on. It only took a minute to warm up, and then Les' fingers were flying over the keys so fast it was hard to keep up. Lily and Greg watched in amazement. In just a minute he had the Porter Industries page open and had accessed their application records.

He frowned when he saw Greg's application had been rejected by Craig Franks. He had put a note on the file saying not a good prospect. Les moved the application to the consideration folder and removed all of Craig's remarks. He put a note on the file stating this person is personally recommended by Lester Hawks. Please give him top consideration for the college training program. He closed the computer with a sigh of satisfaction.

"I have a feeling you are about to be considered for their college training program," Les told Greg.

"How did you do that?" asked Greg. Lily looked like she wanted to ask the same question. Les smiled. My grandfather owns the company and I have spent time working there. I just didn't want to make it my life's work. Craig Franks is an ass. He didn't even consider your application. He probably gave the spot to a friend of his. When you start working there, look out for him. He will stab you in the back if he thinks he can get away with it. Les rubbed his hands together. "How did you tell them to get in touch with you?"

"I gave them my e-mail address," said Greg.

"Les turned the laptop toward him. "Check your mail," he said.

Greg opened his e-mail and looked up in surprise when he saw an e-mail from Porter industries. He opened the letter and read in astonishment. "They want me to come to their offices next week for an interview," he said.

"Tell them you'll be there," said Les.

Greg quickly wrote an acceptance and set it off. He sat back with a stunned look on his face. Then he started thinking. "How am I going to get there? My car quit on me."

"Do you know what's wrong with your car?" asked Les.

"I am not sure, but I think I may have gotten some bad gas," said Greg.

Les took his phone out and called Danny's. He got a hold of Brian. "Do you guys know who we could get to look at Greg's car? He thinks he may have gotten some bad gas."

"Could you send him out to Greg's place to look at the car? Greg has a job interview next week and he needs his car. Thanks Brian."

Les hung up and looked at Greg. Shorty was in Danny's and he will be out in the morning to tow your car in and see what's wrong with it. He won't charge for towing. He will only charge for parts if your car needs any."

Greg looked at Les. "Man, have you ever thought about running for office? I guarantee nobody could do a better job of getting things done than you."

Lily laughed and snuggled closer to Les. "We need to go up and check on Lucky so Lorraine can get away. Greg, you can use the same room you used last night. We will make sure you have a ride to take care of your car in the morning. If you need anything to eat, help yourself."

Les and Lily said goodnight and headed upstairs. When they got to Lily's room, they found Lorraine and Doug snuggled on her love seat, talking.

Doug and Lorraine said goodnight and left. Lily went over and looked at lucky. He was sleeping soundly. There was an empty bottle on the table beside the cradle, so she knew he had been fed. Les came over and put his arm around her and gazed down at his son.

"It won't be long before we have to put him in a crib instead of a cradle," he said.

"Yes," agreed Lily. "He looks like he is growing already. I have Sue's crib, but it is pink. Besides, I want to keep him close as long as possible."

"We'll get him a new crib," said Les. "Every baby deserves their own crib."

Lily shook her head. She snuggled up to Les and hugged him tight. If we have all of the children you were talking about, you'll be glad to let them share a crib," she said laughing. Lily raised her face for his kiss. Les was happy to oblige her. They kissed long and deeply. When they pulled back, they were both shaking and breathless. Lily laid her face against Les and waited to catch her breath.

"Make love to me," she whispered looking up into his eyes.

Les looked at her to see if she was serious. "Are you sure you are ready for this?" he asked.

"I'm sure," said Lily nodding. "I want you to make me fly." She laughed.

Les grinned. "I will see what I can do. One flying Lesson coming right up," he said as he pulled her close and started kissing her again. He stopped briefly to lock the door and help her undress, and then he shed his own clothes and eased her onto the bed. They were very happy Lucky had a nice long sleep.

∽

Les took Greg to meet with Shorty the next morning. While Greg was out of hearing range, behind the car, Les told Shorty to give the car a thorough checking over and to let him know the results. Shorty agreed and hooked the car up and took it to his shop.

Greg wanted to stop by his house, so Les took him by. He told him he had sent a cleaning crew in and had them clean out Erin's room. "I'm glad you did it. I was dreading going back in there," said Greg.

"I wanted to talk to you about your place. I would like to rent it from you and use it to extend Lilly flower fields and maybe add some room for more livestock. I would also like to rent the house and fix it up so, we can use it to house some more workers for the flower fields. I would pay the taxes and other bills that are outstanding. It will give you some spending money while you are training. Porter Industries lets you work while you are training, but the salary will be low at first. Would you be interested in renting?" asked Les.

"Yes, I would," replied Greg. I don't think I could bear to live in the house after this."

"It's better to rent than to sell. You may change your mind later. If you decide to sell, I would like to have first option," said Les.

"You have a deal," said Greg, holding his hand out for Les to shake.

"If you would like to keep anything, it can be stored at my place. I should have my place finished before long and I have a storage shed. After the guys finish there, I will get them started over here."

"I'll look around and see if I need to keep anything. There may be a few things to pass on to Lucky when he gets old enough," said Greg.

They left and headed to town to check in with Shorty. Both were satisfied with the arrangements and the deal they had made.

CHAPTER 10

The day of Jed and Marissa's wedding dawned bright and clear. The sun was shining, and everyone was ready for a happy event. Laura had spent the night with Marissa so she would be there to help her get ready and the two of them had wanted to have a girl's night before Marissa moved on to a new life with Jed.

They were awakened by Marian. She called them to breakfast. The girls were there and very excited to be junior bridesmaids. Laura was going to be her maid of honor. Joe was Jed's best man. Cindy - Marsha and Brian's little girl, was going to be the flower girl. She had insisted Little Sam would be a flower boy, so he was going to walk down the aisle with her and throw flower petals out. He was excited to walk with his new best friend. At the wedding rehearsal, the two youngsters had had everyone teary eyed through their smiles.

Jed had made arrangements for Andy, his brother, to bring his dad to the church and look after him. Sara and Marian had spent the day before decorating the church and preparing everything. They had the bride's bouquet and the bridesmaids' bouquets in cold storage to keep them fresh. The buttonholes for Jed, Joe, Ron, and Gary had been prepared and Joe had insisted on a buttonhole for Andy, too. DD's had also made corsages for Sara and Marian. Everything was ready.

Marissa smiled as she sat still for the hairdresser to arrange her hair. Laura was waiting for her turn after Marissa was done. The girls were very excited. They knew it would not be long before it would be Laura's turn.

Laura looked around at the organized confusion. She smiled. Since getting her sight back, everything looked bright and wonderful. Having to live without her sight taught her to appreciate every moment of seeing everything around her. She sighed. She could not wait for her life with Joe to begin. She had loved him for so long, mostly at a distance. She was ready to get up close and personal. She just had to convince Joe to not worry so much about money. He wanted to provide for her. She understood, but she could help. She was impatient to get started with their life.

She helped Marissa get into her dress and they went downstairs to the ooohs and aaahs of Marissa's family. Marissa's sisters gathered around and showed off their dresses. Then they all piled into the limo to be taken to the church. When they reached the church, they were escorted through a side door into a room where they would not be seen until time to start the wedding.

Jed and Joe were already in another room, waiting. Ron and Andy were with them, waiting until it was time to enter the church.

When everyone was ready, Andy took Ron inside, in his wheelchair, and sat on an outside row. He seated himself on the end of the pew next to him. Marian and Sara had been seated up front. Marian had saved a seat for Saul, who was walking his daughter down the aisle. Jed and Joe took their places up front with the pastor.

When the music started playing, they all turned and watched the doors at the back. First down the aisle were Cindy and Sam. With big smiles on their faces, they threw flower petals down the aisle. When all of their petals were gone, they turned and hurried to where their parents were sitting. Cindy scrambled into Brian's arms and gave her mom a big smile. Sam scrambled into Samuel's arms and smiled at

Crystal, who was seated beside him. The two couples were seated together about half- way down the church isle. Les, Lily and Lucky were next to them and Doug, Lorraine, Karen and Charles were seated in the row in front of them.

The junior bridesmaids came next, followed by Laura. The organist started playing the wedding march and Marissa appeared in the doorway escorted by her dad. They paused for a minute, while everyone stood, then made their way to the front. Marissa was smiling at Jed the whole way. He was smiling back at her, proudly. When Marissa and her dad reached the front, she turned and kissed his cheek then turned back and placed her hand in Jed's hand.

Everyone sat down. Saul went and sat beside Marian. She smiled at him and squeezed his hand. The pastor started the ceremony and, after the I dos, they took the rings from Laura and Joe and placed them on each other's fingers. The pastor pronounced them man and wife and introduced them to the church as Mr. and Mrs. Jed Hillard.

"Now," said the pastor. "The bingo ladies have a surprise for you." He motioned to the double doors to one side and someone opened them. They wanted to show their appreciation for all you have done for them and show their love for you, so, they have arranged a reception for you in the bingo hall.

The pastor turned and led the way to the bingo hall. When they entered, Jed and Marissa stopped and looked around in amazement. The hall had been transformed. There were flowers and ribbons everywhere. There was a big banner saying, "Jed and Marissa Hillard". The tables had been moved back leaving a cleared space in the center for dancing. There was a small stage on one side and some local musicians were up there, getting ready to start playing. At one end of the room there was a table with a large three-tier wedding cake with a bride and groom on top.

Marissa looked around at all of the ladies she had been seeing in bingo each week. "You guys are wonderful," she said tearfully. "This place looks amazing." She started going around hugging the ladies. Jed went right along with her, doing his share of hugging.

The guys in the band started playing and Jed and Marissa took the floor in their first dance as husband and wife. Laura and Joe took a seat at one of the tables and others started finding their seats. Sara helped Andy get Ron settled at one end of a table. She sat on one side and Andy sat on the other. After the first dance, others joined them on the dance floor.

They sat down after the second dance. The young people in the church had volunteered to pass drinks and cake around. There was champagne for the adults and apple juice for the kids. Joe and Laura made toasts, and everyone drank.

Jed and Marissa went to cut the cake, and have it passed around. They wanted to be sure Ron had some cake before he had to leave. He was beginning to look a little tired. They cut the cake and fed each other a bite before turning the knife over to one of the bingo ladies. She was waiting her turn to start cutting for everyone else. Jed and Marissa took their cake to the table and sat down with Ron and Sara. Marissa gave Ron a kiss on his cheek and he patted her hand.

"Welcome to the family," he said.

"Thank you," said Marissa. Kissing him again before sitting beside Jed and leaning against him. She smiled up at him and he leaned forward and kissed her. They had set their cake on the table. They glanced up as Mrs. Hanks, from bingo, placed a box next to them.

"This is the top layer of the cake. You are supposed to eat it on your first anniversary," she said.

"Thank you, Mrs. Hanks. Thank all of you. I loved the surprise," said Marissa.

"We loved doing it," said Mrs. Hanks. She turned and headed back to the cake table after patting Marissa on the shoulder.

After Ron finished his cake, Jed went with him and Andy to help get Ron in the van. Sara decided to go along to help them at home. She kissed Jed and Marissa, and told Marissa she was glad to finally have a daughter. Marissa laughed and hugged her.

Jed and Marissa rejoined the group celebrating with them. They joined the dancers and swayed in each other's arms.

"I'm glad the house is finished enough that we can stay there," said Marissa.

"So am I. I want to have you all to myself. As soon as I find someone to replace Les, I'm going to take you away for a honeymoon," he said.

"Our honeymoon started as soon as we said I do," said Marissa. "It's never going to end."

Jed squeezed her tight. "I love you. I am so glad the mirror helped us find each other. I can't imagine life without you. I don't know how I made it before you. I was just there. Life for me started with you."

Marissa squeezed him back and raised her face for another kiss. Jed was happy to oblige.

Joe and Laura danced by and smiled at Jed and Marissa. Brian and Marsha were dancing with Cindy held up between them. Cindy smiled and waved at Marissa.

"You did a great job with the flowers. You make a beautiful flower girl," said Marissa, smiling at Cindy.

"Sam did good, too," said Cindy.

"Yes, he did," agreed Marissa. "I'll have to be sure and tell him."

Brian and Marsha danced away with a satisfied Cindy. She was happy her little friend was appreciated.

Jed and Marissa went to get another glass of champagne. They wandered over to where Samuel and Crystal were seated with Sam. When they stopped beside them, Jed patted Sam on his shoulder and Marissa smiled at him.

"I wanted to thank you, Sam, for doing such a good job scattering flowers," said Marissa. "You and Cindy did fabulously."

Sam gave her a big grin and ducked his head, shyly. "He loved helping Cindy," said Crystal. "It was a beautiful wedding."

"Thank you for coming," said Marissa. "A wedding is always better when it is celebrated with lots of friends and neighbors."

"We loved seeing so many friendly faces," said Jed. "I hope these friendly faces aren't expecting to see us in the near future."

Marissa hit him on the shoulder and the smiled and hugged him. Samuel and Crystal laughed.

"If they are smart, they should know better," said Samuel. "Congratulations you two and good luck." He stuck out his hand and Jed shook it.

"Thank you," said Jed and Marissa. They wandered on to greet others and thank them for coming. After a while, Jed turned to Marissa.

"I don't think I can stand this for much longer. When can we leave?" he asked.

Marissa looked around. "How about now-?" she said with a smile. She signaled Laura and headed toward the door holding onto Jed's hand. Laura met them at the door.

"Gather the girls. I'm going to toss my bouquet," said Marissa.

Laura called out for all of the single girls to gather around. Marissa closed her eyes and tossed the bouquet over her shoulder. She opened her eyes and turned just in time to see it sail straight into Crystal's arms.

The girls gathered around Crystal and Marissa took this opportunity to slip out of the door with Jed. Laura and Joe followed. When they got outside, Jed stopped suddenly. Marissa looked around to see why he had stopped. She burst out laughing. Jed reluctantly joined in. His truck had streamers of old shoes trailing behind it. Just married was written on the back window.

Jed hurried Marissa over to the truck. "Let's get out of here before they discover we are gone," he said.

Laura and Joe waved them goodbye and went back inside. Jed turned his truck toward the dairy farm and their new home. He stopped just outside of town and untied the streamers of old shoes from the back of the truck and threw them into the bed of his truck.

Marissa grinned at him when he climbed back into the truck and snuggled up as close as she could get with a seat belt on.

CHAPTER 11

Lily decided it was time for her and Lucky to look over their new home. She nestled up to Les and asked him when she was going to pick colors for the rooms.

"We can go over now if you want," said Les grinning at her. He was delighted to see her take an interest in their new home. Instead of going on to the farm, Les turned into the road leading to their new home.

Lily looked around in amazement. The road had been resurfaced and all the wild weeds had been cleared. It looked totally different from the last time she had seen it. Les pulled up in front of the house and stopped. When he helped Lily to get Lucky out of his seat, Les took him and, taking Lily's hand, guided her to the porch.

Lily heard hammering from outside the house and she looked around.

"One part of the crew is working on a barn and corral for Lord George," he said. Lily nodded and let Les guide her inside. The rooms had been cleared and looked much cleaner without the faded old furniture. The floor had been stripped and redone. They went on into the dining room. It looked great. The floors had been done in there also.

The sideboard and china cabinet had been cleaned and polished. Lily ran her hand over the surface. It felt smooth and shone brightly.

They next entered the kitchen. The changes were not as great here, except for some cleaning and leaving spaces for a stove and refrigerator. Most of the room had been left the same, but a new dishwasher had already been installed. The back door opened onto a large glazed patio. The back yard still needed some work done on it, but there were people out there working on it. One of them raised a hand and waved and Les waved back.

They turned around and went back inside. Les showed her the laundry room and pantry. Lily looked at them and then headed for the bedrooms. The first one was empty, clean and waiting to be painted. It had its own bathroom and large walk-in closet.

"I had them take the small bedroom next to this one and turn it into a bathroom and closet," said Les.

Lily smiled. "This is our room. It's great," she said.

They went into the hall and turned the corner. Where there had been a pull-down ladder, there was now a permanent stairway going to the attic. Lily headed up the stairway with Les and Lucky following. When she reached the top, she found a door had been installed. Inside the door she saw a small hallway and two more doors. She opened the door to her right and went inside. There was a spacious room waiting to be painted. To the left were two more doors. She opened one and found a closet. The other door led to a bathroom. The bathroom had another door straight across from the one she had opened. She walked across and found an identical room on the other side. Lily turned and looked at Les. He had been silent during her explorations.

"I thought this would make great rooms for our kids, when they come along," said Les. "There are two more bedrooms downstairs."

Lily walked over and hugged him and Lucky. Les put his other arm around her. Lily raised her lips and kissed him.

"It looks amazing," she said. "You have taken a deserted farmhouse and turned it into a home to last a lifetime. We can be proud to raise a family here." She kissed him again. Les flushed slightly and kissed her, also.

"I was afraid you wouldn't like me doing so much without consulting you," he admitted.

"We have had a lot going on. I'm glad you went ahead and had so much done. It means we can start our lives here sooner," said Lily.

"I'm all for that," said Les with a grin and a kiss. "I should tell you, I rented Greg's place from him. When I get it into shape, I'll hire a couple of more workers to help in the flower fields and they will be able to live in the house and work in the fields"

They started to go down the stairs. Les led the way and Lily followed.

"There is one more thing I have to show you," said Les.

Lily smiled. "What is it?" she asked. Les stopped at the bottom of the stairs and looked at her. "I had the basement remodeled into a game room," he said.

"A game room," she said in astonishment.

"Yes," agreed Les. "It will be perfect for a large pool table my aunt left me."

Lily started laughing. "By all means," she said. "What's a home without a game room? You shouldn't have any trouble getting company. The guys will be lining up when they find out about your pool table."

Les laughed with her. "I would hate for it to go to waste," he said. "It will also provide us with a storm shelter." Lily just chuckled and headed for the door.

"We need to get Lucky home before he needs his bottle. This place is amazing. You have done great." Lily turned and kissed him again before leading the way to the truck. Les followed her, a bright smile on his face.

On the drive to the Smart farm, Lily looked over at Les. He glanced at her and smiled.

"What are you thinking about?" he asked.

"I was wondering if you could get some pictures of your furniture.

If I could get some idea what it looks like, then I would have a better idea what colors to pick for the walls," said Lily.

Les thought about it. "I should be able to get some pictures. I can have my mom look through pictures taken when we visited my aunt. Maybe she could e-mail them to me. I'll check with her as soon as we get Lucky settled down for a nap," said Les.

Les pulled up in front of the house and helped Lily out and then unbuckled Lucky from his seat and carried him inside. Lily started to take him when they entered the door.

"I've got him. Why don't you get his bottle ready?" Les turned and headed for the rocking chair in the corner of the living room.

Lily was back in a few minutes with the bottle and Les got up and let her take his seat in the rocking chair. Lily sat down and started feeding Lucky. He latched on quickly and started sucking greedily. Les laughed. He rubbed his hand gently over Lucky's head. He leaned down and kissed Lilly.

"I'm going to go and call Mom and see about those pictures," he said.

Lily smiled and nodded. She was watching Lucky take his bottle. It was nice to have a baby in her arms again. She wished she could show him to Sue. Sue would have loved being a big sister. Lily shook her head. She would not be sad. After all, she had been able to see Sue on the dreamscape. She had to be thankful for all of her blessings. She had a wonderful man in love with her. She loved him more than she had ever thought possible. She had this beautiful little boy and she saw her baby on the dreamscape. Love was indeed an answer for her.

Les came back into the room, smiling. "Mom said she would see what she could find and send them to me," he said.

He sat down in a chair next to Lily and watched as Lucky finished his bottle and was burped. Lily rocked him for a few minutes, to be sure he was asleep, and then she laid him in his cradle and moved over to sit in Les' lap. She lay back against him and sighed.

"What's wrong?" asked Les.

"Nothing is wrong. I'm just so happy. I want to knock on wood or something to insure nothing changes," she said.

Les held her tightly. "Life is full of changes. Some are good and some hurt. We have to endure the hurtful times to make it to the good times. It all evens out. I think you and I are ready for our good times. I am going to do all in my power to make sure you are happy, but I will hold you tightly during any hurtful times and we can comfort each other," said Les.

"I will be right beside you, making you happy," declared Lily. She lifted her mouth seeking his. Les lowered his lips to hers and kissed her deeply.

Doug came in from tending the horses and smiled at Lily and Les.

"I am going to take a shower before I head to town." He paused for a minute then turned back to face Lily. "Would you have any objection to me asking Lorraine and her kids to move in with us? I don't want to rush her, but I know she has a hard time paying bills and buying groceries."

Lily looked at him and smiled. "I have no objections. I think it's a great idea. Les and I will be moving out as soon as our house is ready. We may be a little crowded until then, but we will work it out. Let me know what she says, and I will see about fixing some rooms up for the kids."

Doug smiled at them both. "Thanks, Sis," he said.

When Doug had gone to take his shower, Lily looked up at Les. "You don't mind having the extra people here, do you?" she asked.

Les shook his head. "No, I like having little ones around. It was the main thing I missed when Mom moved us in with my grandparents. At the reservation there were always a lot of children around. At my grandparent's place everyone was grown. It took a lot of getting used to."

"Is this why you want to have a house full of kids?" asked Lily.

"Maybe, partly, mostly I just want our expressions of love running around all over the place," said Les.

Lily hugged him tightly. "That is beautiful," she said.

Les kissed her.

Doug interrupted them coming back through. "See you later," he said as he waved goodbye. He was very excited about seeing his new love. It had been a long time coming, but finally life was looking good for him and Lily. He was rushing out to grab onto his happiness with both hands. It looked like Lily felt the same way.

Les hugged Lily close. "I think I will just tell Jed to go ahead and get someone else to work the dairy and bring Lord George over here until his stable is finished," he said.

"I think you should. If you are around the workers will get our house done sooner," smiled Lily.

"When do you want to get married?" asked Les. "We don't have to wait until the house is finished."

"Let's get everything straightened out with Jed and find out when your family can come and then set a date," said Lily.

"Alright, we'll get the ring and I'll talk to Jed and call my mom tomorrow. Afterwards we will set a date. Maybe Doug and Lorraine would like to make it a double wedding," suggested Les.

Lily looked at him. She was startled. Then she started smiling. "I'll ask him tomorrow," she said. "Right now, I just want to take Lucky upstairs, and have you make love to me."

Les rose and helped her to stand, "What are we waiting for?" he asked picking up the cradle and heading for the stairs. Lily laughed and followed.

They made love and settled into sleep. They had been sleeping a while when Lily realized she and Les had traveled to the dreamscape together. She looked over and saw Lucky's cradle was there also. She heard a noise and she and Les looked over to where Sue was looking at Lucky. She had a big smile on her face. She reached up and laid a flower in the cradle. She smiled at Lucky one more time and then ran over and hugged Lily and Les.

"Hello, Sweet Sue," said Les rubbing gently on her head. Sue smiled up at him and hugged him. Sue turned to Lily and hugged her tightly. She leaned back and pointed at Lucky. "Brother," she said. Lily nodded with tears showing through her smile. "Yes, he is your brother," she said. Sue smiled again and with one last look at Lucky she faded away.

Lily and Les awakened together back in their bed. Lily looked over and saw Lucky's cradle was where it was supposed to be. Lucky was moving around like he was waking. Both Lily and Les rose up to check on him.

Lily looked down into his cradle and just stared. Les reached in and withdrew the flower lying in his cradle. He handed it to Lily. Lily took the flower and looked up at Les. This flower came from Scotland," she said. "It is not grown in this country. I studied about it when I first started helping my mom with the flower business. It has bell shaped blue flowers on it. There is another just like it with pink shaped flowers. The blue one is called Lucky Laddie and the pink one is called Lucky Lady."

"Wow," said Les.

They stood looking at the flower for a minute until Lucky demanded attention. Les picked him up and Lily turned to go after his bottle. She took the flower with her to get a vase and put it in water. When she came back with the bottle, she brought the flower with her and set it on the dresser.

"I'm going to enjoy it for a few days and then I'm going to dry it and keep it for a keepsake. I'll be able to show it to Lucky when he is older," said Lily sitting down and taking Lucky to feed. Les sat down on the bed and watched her feed Lucky. He glanced over at the flower and smiled.

"Lucky Laddie," he said. "We are the Lucky ones."

Lily smiled and nodded her head in agreement. "Yes, we are."

Lily finished feeding Lucky, burped him, and settled him back in his crib. Lucky went right to sleep. Lily gazed at him for a minute and then she looked at the flower. Les came over and took her in his arms.

"Sue approves of our family. She is happy for us and she loved Lucky," he said.

"I know. I was skeptical about the dreamscape. I thought I may have been imagining it because I wanted to see Sue so badly, but it was real. She was really there. She brought Lucky a flower. I really hugged my baby."

Lily turned into Les' arms and cried. He pulled her close and held her. He was patting her back and making soothing noises. He held her until she quit crying and then he kissed her.

Lily snuggled closer and kissed him back. They settled back into bed and made slow and gentle love to each other.

CHAPTER 12

"Soaring Hawk, you are needed outside. Hurry," said Moon Walking in his head. Les jumped up and grabbed his pants and put them on. He stuck his feet in his boots and headed for the door.

"What is wrong?" asked Lily sitting up.

"I don't know. Moon Walking told me I was needed outside. She said to hurry. You stay here with Lucky. I'll be back as soon as I check it out," he hurried out the door and down the stairs. Lily got up and pulled on a robe.

Les went out onto the porch and looked around. He saw what looked like a bundle of rags lying in the driveway. He saw the lights of Doug's truck coming down the road. Les ran out and stood in the drive and threw his hands up so Doug would see him. Doug slammed on his brakes and got out of his truck.

Les was already bending over the bundle. He turned over a small child gently. He was checking to see if there were any injuries or broken bones. Doug joined him and bent down to help.

"Do you know who he is?" asked Les.

"No, I've never seen him before. I wonder what he is doing here," said Doug. "Thanks for stopping me. I could have run over him. How did you know he was here?"

"Moon Walking told me to hurry outside. I didn't know what was wrong. I just knew to listen to Moon Walking," said Les.

He gently gathered the boy into his arms and headed inside with him. The boy groaned and shifted.

"It's okay, you are safe. We will take care of you," soothed Les.

The boy stilled at the sound of Les' voice. Les took him over and laid him gently on the sofa. They got their first good look at him. Lily had joined them and when she saw the boy, she gasped. Les firmed his mouth and looked like he wanted to punch someone. The boy was covered in bruises. Some were old and some were new.

"Who would do this to a child?" whispered Lily.

"I don't know, but I'm going to find out," said Les. "Doug can you get a doctor to come and check him over; and call the sheriff. We need to find whoever did this and make sure it doesn't happen again. Doug took out his phone and started to make calls.

The boy opened his eyes and looked around. He looked frightened.

"It's okay," soothed Lily. "You are safe, we are going to help you."

"You don't understand," said the boy. "I ran away while they were asleep. I wanted to get help for my mom and myself. Zane is going to kill us both if somebody doesn't stop him. My mom is too scared to do anything, so I knew I had to get help. I just didn't know where to go. I was so weak and tired I couldn't make it to the door."

"What is your name?" asked Lily.

"Jimmy Mays."

"Where do you live?" asked Lily.

"Zane moved us into an old tumble-down shack. I'm not sure where it is. I think part of the time I was going in circles," said Jimmy.

"Who is this Zane character?" asked Les.

"He's just a guy my mom took up with. She has a bad habit of taking up with losers. I tried to keep her from going with him, but she always thinks this time is going to be better. It never is," said Jimmy bitterly.

Les squeezed his shoulder, then drew back fast when Jimmy winced.

Les heard the siren and he and Doug went out to talk to the sheriff. The doctor was pulled in just behind the sheriff's car. Doug directed him to go on inside while he and Les went to talk to the sheriff.

They explained what they knew about the situation. The sheriff looked thoughtful. "I received a report of some squatters in the old Jenkins shack. I just haven't had a chance to check on it. I'll talk to the boy and go see if it's the place."

"You may need some backup. That Zane character sounds like a real bad dude," said Doug.

"It doesn't take much guts to beat on a woman and a child. It is a whole different story when you are facing a grown man with a gun," declared the sheriff.

"Maybe," said Doug. "Just be careful."

"I will," assured the sheriff as they went inside.

The doctor was finishing up as they came in. "He has a lot of bruises, but I think he will be okay. You can bring him by the clinic in a day or so and I will do some x-rays to be sure nothing has been damaged. Otherwise, keep him quiet and feed him. He looks like someone has been trying to starve him."

Jimmy flushed. "Zane wouldn't let us eat until he finished. Usually there wasn't anything left."

Five adults looked away from him to each other. There was fire in all eyes at this treatment of a child. Zane was lucky he was not close enough for any of them to reach. Any of them would have gladly taught him a lesson.

The doctor said goodnight and Doug walked him out, thanking him for coming.

Les and the sheriff came out onto the porch as the doctor drove away.

"Are you sure you wouldn't like us to come along with you?" asked Les.

The sheriff grinned. "I don't want to have to put either of you in jail for assault. Take care of the boy. I'll let you know what I find out." The sheriff entered his car and called on his radio as he was leaving.

Les and Doug watched him drive out of sight. They were worried about him.

Lily fixed a plate of food for Jimmy and added a large glass of milk. She also fixed a plate of snacks for everyone else. She took Jimmy's plate and milk into the living room and placed it on the table in front of the sofa. She helped Jimmy to sit up and then went back for their snack plate. She brought it back and put it on the table next to Jimmy's plate. She sat down on the sofa next to Jimmy and smiled at him.

The child monitor on her belt made a noise, so she rose to check on Lucky. Doug sat down by Jimmy when Lily left. He smiled as he watched Jimmy drink down his glass of milk.

"Eat some food. I'll get you some more milk," he said. He took Jimmy's glass and went to refill it. As he returned with the glass, his phone rang.

"Hello," said Doug.

"This is Sheriff Hayes. It looks like they have been staying here, but Zane must have woken up and discovered the boy gone. It looks like they cleared out in a hurry. I put out an APB on them and I am going to look around here and see if they left anything behind, keep your guard up, just in case they come by there looking for the boy."

"Okay, Sheriff, we'll keep watch. Thanks for calling. Let us know what you find out," said Doug.

"Okay," said the sheriff.

Doug turned to Les, who was sitting in a chair watching Jimmy and listening.

"Sheriff Hayes said the shack was empty. They must have found Jimmy missing and taken off. He said to keep watch in case they come by here looking for him," said Doug.

"My mom is gone," said Jimmy tearfully.

"The sheriff is looking for them and he has other police looking, too. We just have to hope he finds them," said Doug.

Jimmy hung his head and stopped eating, "I didn't mean to lose my mom. I was looking for help. I wasn't running out on her," said Jimmy.

"This isn't your fault," said Les. "You were trying to help your mom the only way you knew how. Give the sheriff a chance to find her."

"What's going to happen to me if he doesn't find my mom? I don't have anyone else," said Jimmy looking scared.

"Don't borrow trouble. You will be alright. We will make sure of it. You are not alone," said Doug.

Lily came back down with Lucky and handed him to Les while she went to get him a bottle. When she came back with the bottle, she took Lucky and settled into the rocking chair to feed him. She looked at Jimmy, who was sitting there looking upset and not eating.

"Why aren't you eating?" she asked Jimmy.

Jimmy looked down at his plate and then glanced at Lily. "I'm sorry, I don't think I can eat any more right now," he said.

Lily shook her head and frowned. "Your stomach must have shrunk. Just wait a while and then you can eat a little more. If you get hungry, let me know. We will have to give you small meals," she smiled at Jimmy.

Jimmy looked at Lucky busy sucking on his bottle. "Is that your baby?"

"Yes, his name is Lucky," replied Lily.

Jimmy smiled. "He sure is lucky."

Lily smiled back at him. "I think we are the lucky ones."

They heard a car stop out front and both men got up to see who it was. Sheriff Hayes was coming to the door. They stood aside and let him in. He looked over at Jimmy and smiled to see him sitting up and eating. He walked over and sat next to him on the sofa. Jimmy looked at him curiously.

"Have you found my mom?" he asked.

"Not yet, but we are still looking. I found this picture at the shack where you had been staying," said Sheriff Hayes. He held the picture up so Jimmy could look at it.

Jimmy eagerly took the picture and gazed at it. "It's my dad," he said. "I never met him; he died before I was born. My mom told me he was a soldier and he died in the war. This picture is all I have of him. I had to hide it to keep Zane from tearing it up."

Sheriff Hayes looked at the picture and then at Jimmy. He shook his head.

Doug and Les had been watching him closely. "Do you know the man in the photo?" asked Les.

"Yes, he is my younger brother. He died in service about eight and a half years ago. If I'm right, Jimmy is his son and that would make him my nephew." He looked at Jimmy. "I want to find out if I am your uncle. I want to take a swab and send it to the lab and have them check and see if we are related. Is it alright with you, Jimmy?"

Jimmy shrugged his shoulder. "Sure," he said. Sheriff Hayes got out a plastic bag and a cotton swab. He ran the swab around inside of Jimmy's mouth and then enclosed it in the bag. He put the bag into his pocket and rose from the sofa. He looked down at Jimmy.

"I will let you know if I find your mom. You will be safe here. Just don't go outside without someone with you and listen to Lily, Les, and Doug. They will watch out for you. Okay?" he asked.

"Okay," agreed Jimmy.

Doug and Les rose and walked out with Sheriff Hayes.

Sheriff Hayes turned and looked at them when they were outside. "It makes me furious to think Alec had a son and his mother didn't let us know. We could have helped her out and my nephew would not be sitting in there all bruised up, starved and scared to death. I see all kinds in this job, but this time it really hits close to home. I really hope we find her, but if Jimmy is my nephew, he is not going anywhere with her," Sheriff finished grimly.

Doug put his hand on Sheriff Hayes' shoulder in comfort.

"Let us know if there is anything we can do to help." he said.

"Just keep Jimmy safe," said Sheriff Hayes.

"We will," promised Les and Doug. They watched Sheriff Hayes get into his car and drive off before he looked around and went back inside. Les made sure the door was locked when they went in.

"You check upstairs and I'll check down here. Make sure all windows and doors are locked," said Les to Doug. Doug nodded and they left to look around and see to the safety of everyone inside. Les and Doug met up downstairs a short time later. They nodded to each other and went into the living room.

Jimmy was nodding off on the sofa. Lily was burping Lucky and she smiled as she rose to take Lucky up to his cradle.

"Jimmy needs a bath, but he is just so tired, we can wait until morning. Can one of you bring him upstairs? You can put him in the bedroom with the twin beds." Lily directed.

Les came over and gently lifted Jimmy and carried him upstairs. Lily followed him into the room. He took off Jimmy's worn out shoes and settled him under the covers. Jimmy settled with a sigh and didn't wake up until the next morning.

Les and Lily went out. They left the door open a little and left a light on in the hall. They did not want Jimmy to wake up and be scared.

Lily took Lucky and settled him in his cradle. "We really are going to have to get Lucky a larger bed, soon," she said. "He is getting bigger every day." She got him settled and went into Les' arms. He leaned down and kissed her.

"Why don't you lie down and try to catch a nap. I'll go down and help Doug keep watch," said Les. He kissed her again.

"Okay," agreed Lily with a yawn. Les grinned. "Sleep," he said leading her toward the bed.

"I will," promised Lily. She crawled into the bed and was asleep almost before her head touched the pillow. Les took the child monitor and clipped it to his belt before leaving the room.

He found Doug sitting on the sofa, eating the snacks Lily had left for them. Les took Jimmy's plate and glass into the kitchen and put the glass in the dishwasher. The plate he covered and put in the refrigerator. He got both himself and Doug a glass of tea and headed back to the living room. He handed Doug his glass and sat down and started eating some of the snacks.

"Thanks," said Doug taking a large drink of tea.

"Did Lorraine agree to move in?" asked Les.

"Yes, she wants to talk to the kids and prepare them. She said to give them a couple of days to pack. I thought I could store her furniture in my garage until she decides what to do with it." He reached into his pocket and brought out a jewelry box. "I bought her a ring. I thought I would wait until they get moved in and then give it to her." He opened the box and showed the ring to Les.

"Nice," said Les. "I haven't bought Lily a ring, yet. I keep thinking I'll take her by and let her pick it out, but things keep happening and we haven't had a chance to go by the jewelry store."

"Yes," agreed Doug. "Things have livened up around here. You must be our wake-up call."

Les laughed. "I don't know about a wake-up call, but we have not had a dull moment since the mirror sent me to Lily."

Doug's phone rang. "Hello," he said.

"We caught him," said Sheriff Hayes. "He was at a gas station and when he went inside one of my deputies pulled up to get some gas. He noticed a woman slumped over in the front seat. When he got a good look at her he saw she was covered in bruises. Zane came out and when he saw the deputy looking in his car, he started to run. My deputy called for him to halt and when he didn't stop my deputy shot at him. He didn't hit him, but Zane stopped and put his hands up. The deputy called for backup, cuffed him and put him in the back of his patrol car. He checked on the woman and she was unconscious, so he called for an ambulance. They took her to the hospital. I'm going to check on her now. I'll let you know how she is when I find out. How is Jimmy doing?"

"He's sleeping. Les and I have been keeping watch. I guess we can get some sleep now," thanks for calling," said Doug.

"Get some sleep. I'll call back in the morning," said Sheriff Hayes.

They hung up and Doug filled Les in on all the sheriff had said.

Les nodded. "It's too bad the deputy didn't aim better," he said.

Doug laughed. "Yeah," he agreed. They took the plate and glasses to the kitchen and turned off the lights and headed upstairs to sleep. They were relieved not to have to worry about Zane, for now.

Les undressed and slipped in beside Lily. She nestled close and opened her eyes. "Sleep, it's all over. The sheriff has them."

"Okay," said Lily closing her eyes and going back to sleep. Les grinned and held her close while he prepared to join her. First, he closed his eyes and thought about Moon Walking. "Thank you, Grandmother," he said.

"You are welcome, Grandson," said Moon Walking.

CHAPTER 13

The next morning, Les headed for town. He stopped off and purchased a horse trailer and an outfit for Jimmy. Les didn't know what size shoes Jimmy took, but He picked up a pair which looked about right. Anything was better than what he had been wearing. Les drove on to the Hillard dairy farm. When he arrived, they were finishing up with milking, so he went inside and there he found Jed getting ready to leave. He filled him in on everything happening about Jimmy.

"I didn't know Alec had a son. I think someone mentioned something about him being married, but nothing else," said Jed.

"They didn't know. Evidently, this Peggy Mays took back her maiden name and even called Jimmy, Mays instead of Hayes. She didn't let anyone in the family know about Jimmy. The poor kid thought he was all alone if anything happened to his mother. He's one brave little fellow to try to find help all by himself, when he did not even know where he was. He was very weak also. The guy they were with had him half-starved." Les shook his head.

"I'm glad he found help with you guys. You should open a lost and found agency. It seems you attract people in need of help," laughed Jed.

"Yeah, it seems that way," agreed Les. "I came by so I could clean out my room and pick up Lord George. I'll keep him at the farm until I get his stall finished. I want to get my room cleaned out so you will have it for a new helper. Have you found anyone, yet?" asked Les.

"Not so far, I've put word out, but had no one apply for the job," said Jed.

"If I hear of anyone, I'll send them your way," promised Les.

"Thanks, good luck. I'm sorry to lose you, but I understand. Maybe everything will settle down and you and Lily can start the new life both of you deserve," Jed stuck his hand out to shake Les' hand. Les shook his hand and went to load up Lord George. Then he cleaned out his room. There was not a lot of stuff there. Les had always traveled light. He then headed to the farm.

When he arrived, he unloaded Lord George into the corral he had been in before and went in to find Lily making breakfast. He went over and kissed her.

"Good morning beautiful," he said. Lily grinned at him and told him to get his coffee. Breakfast was almost ready. Les looked at the table and found Jimmy sitting there grinning at him. Lily had rubbed cream on his bruises, and he was looking a little better. At least they did not look as painful. Lily had also made sure he had a bath. He was sitting there in a tee shirt of Doug's. Les handed him his new clothes and told him to try them on. Jimmy looked in the bag and then went into the hall and switched his clothes. When he came back, he had a proud smile on his face, and he came over and hugged Les.

"Thanks, I haven't had any new clothes in years. The clothes I was wearing, my mom got them from a box at a church. I don't think I have ever had anything just for me." He rubbed the sleeve of his shirt. It was like he wanted to feel the newness.

Les looked at Lily and she looked away to hide the tears in her eyes.

"I'm glad to see they fit pretty good. I had to guess at the size. I see you are feeling better this morning," said Les.

"I'm okay. Mrs. Lily told me they had Zane in jail and my mother in the hospital," said Jimmy.

"Yes, I haven't heard anything this morning. I went to pick up my things and collect Lord George," said Les.

"Who is Lord George?" Jimmy asked.

"He's my horse. I had him at the place where I was working. Since I am not going to work there any more, I brought him here temporarily until I get his stable built."

Lily came in and set their plates on the table. Lucky made a shuffling sound in his cradle. Les went over and checked on him, but he had gone back to sleep. Les filled two cups with coffee and brought Jimmy a glass of orange juice. Lily brought in the final plate as Doug came in the back door.

"Get your coffee, breakfast is on the table," called Lily. Les held her chair so Lily could be seated and took his own seat. Doug came into the dining room with his coffee in hand and went to his seat. They all bowed their heads and Doug said a prayer.

"Let's eat, I'm starved," said Doug.

"You are always starved," said Lily teasingly.

"I see you have brought Lord George back," said Doug.

"Yes, temporarily until I get his stable ready," agreed Les.

"Doug," said Lily. "How would you feel about having a double wedding with me and Les? Do you think Lorraine would go for it?" asked Lily.

"I don't know, but I will ask her. I think it is a great idea. Anything to speed up things, I'm all for. I am ready to start my life with Lorraine and the kids. I'm thinking about adopting her kids if they will go for it. I haven't talked to her about it, yet. I was just thinking about it," said Doug. He looked like he wished he hadn't said anything about it. It had slipped out.

"Don't worry, we won't say anything. You and Lorraine have to work it out between you," Lily assured him.

"Thanks," said Doug relieved.

Jimmy had been sitting there quietly listening to them talk. He looked like he was enjoying a taste of normal family life. Les looked at Jimmy and grinned.

"How would you like to play a game on the Play Station, when you finish breakfast?" asked Les.

Jimmy looked sad. I've never played on Play Station," he said.

Les shook his head. "I'll teach you. I'll have you playing like a champ in no time," he said.

Jimmy grinned. "I have always wanted to learn," he said.

"Okay," said Les. "What are we waiting for? Just remember it's not nice to beat your teacher."

"Don't pay any attention to him, Jimmy. You beat the pants off him," said Doug.

Les and Jimmy went to the living room with Lily and Doug's laughter following them.

Lily cleaned up the kitchen and Doug went back out to work. Jimmy was learning the basics of Play Station. Les was an expert at it and a very good teacher. He soon had Jimmy competing like a pro. Lily listened to their voices and grinned. It seemed as if Jimmy was having a good time.

Lily picked up Lucky's cradle and headed for the front room. The doorbell rang just as she was passing it. Les looked over and watched as she opened the door. There was an older couple at the door. They looked vaguely familiar, but Lily couldn't place them.

"Hello, can I help you?" asked Lily.

The man stepped forward and held out his hand. "I'm Aaron Hayes and this is my wife Sandra. My son Alvin told me about Alec's son being here. We had to come out and see for ourselves."

"Please come in. You are Sheriff Hayes' parents. I didn't know the sheriff had gotten the results of the test back," said Lily. She stood back so they could come inside.

"I don't know if he has or not. I had to come and see my grandson," said Sandra.

They came on in and spotted Jimmy sitting on the sofa. Les stood up when they came in. Sandra and Aaron came on over and looked at Jimmy. Sandra drew in a quick breath. She was upset to see all the bruises on Jimmy. She blinked her eyes to keep from crying. Aaron was made of sterner stuff. Aaron had been the sheriff for many years until he retired, and his son took on the job. Aaron was able to look past the bruising and see the boy behind them.

"I don't need a test," Aaron said. "Jimmy is our grandson. He looks just like my boys did when they were his age." Aaron went over and knelt in front of Jimmy. He held out a hand to him and when Jimmy put his hand in his, Aaron pulled him into a hug. "I'm your grandpa, Jimmy and this is your grandma," he pointed at Sandra. "I'm sorry we haven't been around to get to know you. But we didn't know about you. If your mother had let us know about you, we would have taken care of you both."

"You're really my grandpa and grandma?" asked Jimmy.

"Yes, we are," said Sandra. "We would like for you to come and live with us. You can meet all of your cousins and your aunts. You have already met your Uncle Alvin. We can show you pictures and tell you all about your dad."

"I have cousins," marveled Jimmy.

"Yes, your Aunt Lori has two little girls and your Aunt Randi has two girls. Your Uncle Alvin has a boy and a girl. You will have a lot of children to play with. Would you like to live with us?" asked Sandra.

Jimmy looked from one to the other, thinking. "What about my mom? Can she come, too?" he asked.

Aaron glanced at Sandra. "When your mom gets well, we will discuss it with her and see what she wants to do," said Aaron.

"Okay," said Jimmy. "I would like to go with you and meet my family, and I want to learn all about my dad."

Aaron looked at Les and Lily. "It is alright for him to go with us. I talked to the judge and he gave us temporary custody of him."

Lily nodded and came over and gave Jimmy a hug. "If you ever need us, you just let us know. It has been a pleasure to meet you, Jimmy."

Les pulled him into a hug also. You keep up on your Play Station. You are doing great. Maybe we can get together for another game sometime," he said.

"I would like that," said Jimmy. "Thank you all for taking care of me."

Jimmy took his grandma's hand and left with them. He turned as he was going out the door and smiled and waved at them.

Lily turned into Les' arms and he held her close. "He is going to be alright. He will be surrounded by a loving family. In time he will put these awful memories behind him," said Les.

"I know," said Lily. "I'm glad for him. I'm just going to miss him."

"Yeah, me, too," agreed Les.

Doug came in the back door and on into the living room.

"Who was Jimmy leaving with?" he asked.

"His grandparents," said Lily. "They are Sheriff Hayes' parents. Jimmy wanted to go with them, and they had a paper from the judge giving them temporary custody."

"It will be good for Jimmy to be a part of a loving family," said Les.

"Yes," agreed Doug. "I am turning the horses over to my helpers and taking the rest of the day off. I think I will see what Lorraine thinks about a double wedding. Why don't you two get out and go jewelry shopping before anything else happens?"

"We will as soon as I show some pictures of my furniture to Lily so she can tell me what colors she wants our house to be painted inside. The sooner the painters get started, the sooner we can move in," Les pulled Lily into a hug and kissed her.

Doug left and Les opened his laptop and pulled up the pictures from his mom. Lily sat on the sofa next to him and studied the pictures. "This is lovely furniture," she said. "What are you going to do with the piano?"

"We can store it in one of the downstairs bedrooms temporally, until later. I am going to have a combination Library, Music room added on later, but I want what we have finished first so we can move in. We may want to add some other rooms, but we can decide about it later," said Les.,

Lily was sitting there, listening to him talk, in amazement. She turned back to the pictures and started studying them again. She looked through all the pictures and the pulled forward a paper and pen. She talked while she was writing.

"I think the living room, the hall, and the dining room should be soft rose beige. The kitchen should be sea foam green and the cabinets should be stained to match the side- board and china cabinet. The master bedroom, closet, and bath need to be pale sky blue. The upstairs bedrooms should be mist green and ivory. The other two bedrooms should also be ivory. I want the outside to be white with black trim." Lily handed Les the paper and smiled. Les took it, folded it and put it in his pocket.

"Let's get ready to go. We can drop this off on the way to town," said Les. While Lily went to prepare Lucky for a trip to town, Les took out the list and made another copy of it to keep. He wanted to make sure Lily had things just the way she wanted them.

They decided to go to town in Lily's van so they could pick up a few groceries. Lily handed Les the keys. Les grinned and helped her get Lucky settled. Les stopped by their house and took the color list in and gave it to the workers.

When they arrived in town, Les headed for the jewelry store. They went in and while they were looking at rings, the ladies behind the counter came around and made a fuss over Lucky. Lucky laid there looking up at them, as if he was wondering why all these women were hovering over him.

Les grinned. "Just you wait, Lucky. In a few years you will appreciate the attention more."

Lily slapped him on the arm. "Be nice," she said.

"I'm always nice," whispered Les.

They had been looking at all the rings, but Les noticed Lily's eyes kept wandering back to a certain ring. It was a pale blue color surrounded by Small diamonds. It had a platinum setting. The center stone was raised slightly, and he diamonds around it were formed in the shape of a star.

"Can we see this one?" asked Les pointing to the ring.

The clerk brought the ring out and handed it to Les. Les took Lily's hand and slid the ring on her finger. It was a perfect fit.

"Do you like it?' asked Les.

Lily held up her hand and gazed at it. She turned her hand side to side and watched it sparkle. "I love it," she said. She raised her face for a kiss. Les leaned forward and kissed her.

"We will take this and the matching bands," said Les.

The clerk took his card and went to ring up their purchase. Lily and Les kissed again. He held her close, with Lucky held between them.

The clerk brought them the bag with the wedding bands along with the receipt and thanked them for shopping with them.

Lily and Les started for the grocery store. They quickly gathered what they needed and packed them in the van. They spotted Doug's truck at Danny's, so they stopped and went in. Doug was at the bar talking to Lorraine. They sat on stools next to him and said hello to Lorraine. Lorraine was wearing an engagement ring also. The girls admired each other's rings, while the guys watched them indulgently.

"Did you ask Lorraine about the double wedding?" Lily asked looking at Doug.

"Yes, he did. I think it is a great idea. I see no reason to go to the expense of two weddings in such a short amount of time," said the ever-practical Lorraine.

CHAPTER 14

"Now all we have to do is find out what dates are good for your family and talk to the pastor about the church. Then Lorraine and I can go looking for dresses," said Lily. Lily looked at Les with a smile.

Les squeezed her hand.

Les' phone dinged and he opened it to find a text message from Greg. He read the message and smiled with satisfaction.

"Greg has been accepted into the training program at Porter Industries. He has been set up in a company apartment with two roommates, who are also in the program. He will be taking classes in the mornings and working with a trainer in the afternoons. He is very excited and thanks everyone for giving him this chance."

"We didn't do very much," said Doug. "Les was the one to get him a chance at a job he wanted. If I am ever in a bind, it will be nice to know you are part of my family and we can depend on you," Doug assured Les.

Les smiled at all of them. "I am very happy to be a part of this family. I haven't felt this accepted since before Mom moved us away from the reservation."

Les pulled out his phone. "Let's see when we can have this wedding.

Hello, Mom, we are planning to have a double wedding in about a week. Lily's brother Doug and his fiancée, Lorraine, are going to be married in the same ceremony. Do you want me to make reservations for you and the grandparents at the bed and breakfast?"

"You sure don't give much notice. Don't forget to get a room for our chauffeur, Simpson," said Elaine.

"Alright, Mom, I'll make the reservations for next weekend. I love you," said Les.

"One down one to go," said Les. "Hello, Pastor Franks, this is Les Hawks. I was wondering if it would be possible to get the church and you for a double wedding next weekend."

"It's for myself and Lily and her brother, Doug, and his fiancée, Lorraine."

"Great, I'll have Lily call you in a couple of days with all the details," said Les.

He looked at everyone and smiled at their looks of amazement. "He said we could have the church next Saturday at 3 o'clock and he would be happy to perform the ceremony."

"Wow," said Brian. He had been standing behind the counter listening to them talk. "I have never seen a wedding planned so easily or so fast."

Lily turned and looked at Lorraine. "There is a bridal boutique just down the street. Why don't we go and see if we can find dresses we like?"

"Sure," said Lorraine. She looked over at Brian and he waved his hand for her to go. She hung up her apron and came over to Lily.

"Why don't you leave Lucky with us while you look for dresses?" asked Les.

Lily looked at him uncertainly. "Are you sure?" she asked.

"Yes, we are grown men. We can handle one little baby," assured Les. Doug and Brian nodded agreement.

"Ok," said Lily. "We won't be long."

BETTY MCLAIN

"Take your time. We will be fine," said Les. He handed her his credit card and quietly told her to get Lorraine and Karen's dresses, also. Then he leaned over to kiss her and took Lucky's carry seat.

Lorraine kissed Doug and the two ladies left to go and find the perfect dress. Lily glanced back at the door and saw all three guys surrounding Lucky, talking to him. She grinned and followed Lorraine out of the door.

Lily and Lorraine arrived back at Danny's about two hours later. They stopped just inside the door, amazed to see all the guys sitting at tables close to Les, watching Les with Lucky. Lucky's seat was in the middle of the table and Les had him on his shoulder. Danny had taken the bottle to the kitchen for Barry to warm. When Barry brought it back to Les, he and Danny had stayed and watched Les feed Lucky. Several other guys had come in as well. They all watched as Les fed Lucky and was now burping him. Lucky let out a large burp. All the guys cheered and laughed. Les was smiling. Lily and Lorraine laughed. Les looked over at Lily and smiled at her.

"Look Lucky, Mommy is back." said Les.

Lily made her way over to the table and, leaning forward, gave Les a kiss. She then kissed Lucky on top of his head. Les looked at the bags Lily and Lorraine were carrying and smiled again.

"Did you find what you were looking for?" he asked.

"Yes, we did," said Lily. She looked at Lorraine who was leaning on the back of Doug's chair with her arms around his neck. Her bags were lying on the table in front of him. He pulled her around to sit in his lap.

"We are all set. Did you guys enjoy yourselves?" asked lily

"We had a blast. Lucky entertained the whole place," said Les. Lucky just looked up at him sleepily. "I called Mrs. Glass and made reservations for my family for next weekend. I called Mom back and let her know, so we are all set. I told her to have Granddad send the furniture in three days."

"Are you sure the house will be ready by then?" asked Lily.

"Yes, the painters should be done by late tomorrow. We give them one day to lay carpet. They still have one day to finish up any loose ends," said Les. "The stable for Lord George will be finished by tomorrow, but I will wait until we move in to move him."

"Great," said Lily, smiling happily. "Now all I have to do is harvest the flowers to decorate the church."

Les looked around at the men sitting at tables watching. "If any of you know of anyone looking for work, have them get in touch. Jed needs someone at the dairy, and we are going to hire more help for Lily with the flower harvesting, Doug could use another helper with his horses so he can take a little time off."

"I think my sister's oldest son is looking for work," said one of the guys. "I'll let him know."

"Thanks," said Les nodding.

"What are you going to do since you are no longer at the dairy?" asked Brian.

"As soon as Lily and I get back from our honeymoon, I'm going to start working on some ideas I have for new software games. I can work from home on the computer and send my work to Porter Industries. I don't have to be at the factory," said Les.

"Will they let you do that?" asked Brian.

"I am one of the stockholders. My mom and granddad are the other stockholders. Granddad will be glad to have me working for the company again," said Les.

"We need to get Lucky home so he can rest," said Lily.

They gathered up Lily's bags along with Lucky and all of his things and headed for the van. They had no idea at the stunned silence they left behind in Danny's. The men sat looking at each other.

Brian looked at Doug. "Did you know your new brother-in-law was a millionaire?" he asked.

Doug shook his head. "I knew he had money, but I had no idea he was part owner of Porter Industries. It doesn't matter. He is still just a great guy and he makes my sister happy."

Everyone was nodding their agreement.

In the van, Lily was sitting in the middle, leaning against Les.

"Tired?" he asked.

"Yeah, shopping is so much more tiring than working with flowers," she said.

Les laughed. "You enjoy working with flowers. Shopping is a chore."

"You and Doug are going to have to take Charles and get him outfitted for the wedding," said Lily.

"We will," assured Les. "I was thinking about the back bedroom. It is large so even after we store the piano in there, I should have enough room to fix up an office and set up some computers. I'll even have room for a playpen. I would be able to work in there and watch Lucky while you are working with the flowers."

"Are you sure you want to handle a small child and work?" asked Lily.

"We can try it out and if it doesn't work, we will try something else," said Les.

"Okay," agreed Lily.

They arrived home and Les carried Lucky while lily carried her bags and Lucky's diaper bag inside.

Lily hung her dress inside her closet, still in its bag. She smiled when she thought how beautiful she had felt when she tried it on.

Les came up behind her and encircled her with his arms. Lily leaned back against him. She loved the feel of his arms around her.

"I called my cousin Alex and asked if we could visit them for a couple of days after we are married. I want you to meet his family and I want you to meet Moon Walking," said Les.

"I would love to visit your family and I am looking forward to meeting Moon Walking," said Lily. She turned in his arms and taking his hand led him to their bed. After a quick look to be sure Lucky was alright, they discarded their clothes and she pulled back the covers and crawled into the bed. Les was quick to join her.

After Doug and Lorraine left, Brian called Marsha and told her about the upcoming wedding. She called Marissa and Laura and informed them. She told Marissa to let Jed know. She started planning a party for Lily and Lorraine. Brian talked to Danny, who agreed to have a bachelor party for Les and Doug. Marsha also arranged for some of their friends to take Lily's flowers, after she gathered them, and decorate the church for the wedding.

The next morning arrived with a bang. Doug was moving Lorraine and her kids into the farmhouse. Les and Lily had slept in. They went back to sleep after Lucky's middle of the night feeding. The noise woke them, and they quickly dressed and went to help. Lily showed them which rooms to use and then she went to start breakfast as Les and Doug carried in boxes and bags.

Karen and Charles were carrying in some of their toys in bags. They were very excited to be moving to the farm. Les and Doug carried Karen's vanity up to her room. After all, the boxes were unloaded and put into the rooms they were supposed to go in, they started unpacking the boxes.

"Leave the unpacking until after eating," said Doug. "Lily has breakfast ready."

Everyone quickly stopped what they were doing and headed for the dining room. They found Lily putting food on the table and Les was giving Lucky his bottle.

"Everyone sit down and eat," said Lily with a smile. "You will have more energy for unpacking after filling your stomach."

"It looks great," said Lorraine. "You don't have to cook for us all the time."

"We can take turns. It's just until Les and I get moved into our house," said Lily.

"Well, you cooked so we will clear up after we eat," said Lorraine.

"Ah, Mom," said Charles.

Lorraine gave him a stern look. "You know you have to help out. I don't want any complaining."

"Besides," said Doug. "After we get everything cleaned and put away and boxes unpacked and put up, we can go and check on the horses. Maybe you can help me feed them. Would you like that?"

Charles and Karen both nodded excitedly and continued eating. Lorraine gave Doug a smile and squeezed his hand. He smiled back.

Les finished burping Lucky and put him in his cradle. He came over and started to get himself a plate, but Lily handed him one piled with food. She had put it aside for him. He leaned down and kissed her then sat down beside her and started eating.

"When are you going to start working on the software game you were talking about last night?" Doug asked Les.

"I'll probably wait until we get moved into our house and I can get an office set up," replied Les. "I have started putting a few ideas down on my laptop. I just need to flesh them out and put them together."

He looked at Charles and Karen. "Do you two know how to play on Play Station?" he asked.

"Charles is good on it, but I don't do as good," said Karen.

"When I get the game ready, I might get you two to test it for me before I send it in," said Les.

"You mean I would get to play the game before anyone else!" exclaimed Charles.

"Yes," said Les.

"Cool," said Charles.

Everyone laughed at his response. They finished eating and Lily took Lucky upstairs to let him sleep some more. Charles and Karen started helping Lorraine gather dishes and take them into the kitchen. They soon had the dishwasher loaded and ran to their rooms to put away their things. Doug drew Lorraine into his arms and kissed her before going outside to check on the horses. Lorraine finished cleaning the dining room and went to unpack her things.

Lily received a call from Marsha. She wanted to know if they could get together with Lorraine and a few of the girls for a small pre-wedding party. She said they would bring the food and if they brought it to the farm, they could bring the kids and they would have plenty of room to play. Lily called Lorraine in and asked her what she thought about it. Lorraine said it was fine with her.

"Lorraine said okay. When do you want to come?" asked Lily.

"Will day after tomorrow at 4 o'clock in the afternoon be okay?" said Marsha. "I'll be off work then."

"Okay," agreed Lily.

She started to go down and tell the guys, but met them coming in.

"Brian called and wants Doug and I to come into Danny's day after tomorrow for a guy get together," said Les.

Lily laughed. "Marsha called me for the same reason, only they are coming here and bringing food."

Les and Doug laughed. "We should have expected it," said Doug.

"Do you need us to get anything or to help get ready?" asked Les.

"I'll let you know when I have time to think about it," said Lily.

"Okay," said the guys as they turned to go back outside.

"I'm going to exercise Lord George," said Les.

"Have fun," said Lily. Lorraine just smiled and followed Doug out so she could get another kiss.

CHAPTER 15

The night of the party, the guys headed for town and Lily and Lorraine prepared to be invaded. Marsha, Marissa and Laura arrived first. Lily and Lorraine helped them carry food into the kitchen. Crystal and Sara came next with more food. They were followed by Marian Embers and Mary Sands. They, also, brought more food and drinks.

"We have enough food to feed the whole town," remarked Lorraine.

"We have more ladies coming. We wanted to be sure we had enough," declared Laura.

Lily slipped upstairs to check on Lucky. While she was there, she called Les.

"Hi, Love, aren't you supposed to be partying?" asked Les.

"The ladies are downstairs getting the food ready," said Lily. "They brought enough food to feed an army and I was wondering."

"What were you wondering?" asked Les patiently.

"Why don't you guys get together and join us at the farm. Bring some drinks and bring the whole crowd. It is silly to have two parties when it would be more fun for all of us together."

Les thought for a minute. "I think you are right. Let me run it by the guys. I think the food will convince them," said Les. "If I don't call you back, you can expect us."

"Okay," said Lily, happily hanging up the phone.

Lily clipped the monitor on her belt and went back downstairs. She didn't let on about the guys coming. She thought it would be a nice surprise.

Meanwhile, in town a stretch limo had pulled into the parking lot of the bread and breakfast. Les' mom had called and extended their stay there to include extra days. She had decided she wanted to meet Lily and Lucky before the wedding. Les' grandparents were with her. When they checked in, Mrs. Glass mentioned the big party at the farm. Elaine got directions to the farm. She had Simpson take their bags to their rooms, then, they headed for the farm.

The guys arrived at the farm first. After a moments surprise, the group was welcomed, and everyone started filling plates and enjoying themselves. Les made his way over to Lily and kissed her.

"Great idea," he said.

"I thought so," agreed Lily smiling.

"Hey, Doug," called Brian looking out the window. "You have a limo pulling into your yard."

"What?" said Doug going to look. He saw the driver get out and open the door for an elegantly dressed woman. He then opened another door and two older people exited the limo.

"Les, I think you have company," said Doug grinning.

Les came over to see. When he saw who was out there, he hurried to the door. He hurried down the steps and over to his mom. He gave her a hug and turned to his grandparents. He hugged each of them and turned back to his mom.

"I'm glad you came early," he said. "You'll get a chance to meet everyone before the wedding."

"I wanted to meet Lily and my grandson," said Elaine.

"So, do I," agreed Mallory Porter.

"Well, come inside," said Les taking their arms and guiding them forward. There was quite a crowd standing on the porch, watching. They had come out to see who had arrived in a limo.

Les stopped when he was next to Simpson and put out his hand. Simpson shook his hand with a smile.

"It's nice to see you, Les," he said.

"It's nice to see you, too. Come inside and join the party. We have plenty to eat and I want you to meet my family," said Les.

Simpson fell into step with Mr. Porter behind Les and the ladies.

When Les saw Lily on the porch, he guided Elaine and Mallory over to where she was. He reached over and pulled her to his side.

"Lily, this is my mom, Elaine and my Grandma, Mallory. Ladies, this is the love of my life, Lily," said Les.

Elaine reached over and hugged her and then Mallory gave her a hug also. "I'm very glad to meet you, Lily," said Elaine. "Now, where's my new grandson?" Lilly laughed. "He's upstairs asleep." Just then there was a sound from the baby monitor. "Maybe not," said Lily. "Would you like to go with me to get him?"

"Lead the way," said Elaine as she and Mallory followed Lily inside and upstairs to see Lucky.

Les ushered Jacob Porter and Simpson inside and introduced them around.

They visited and talked with people. Jacob was very interested in meeting Doug and Lorraine. Finally, Les and his granddad made themselves plates and sat down to talk.

"I was wondering how you were coming along on the game you were working on," said Jacob.

"I still have a little tweaking to do, but it is almost ready," said Les"

"What's it about?" asked Jacob.

"It's an obstacle course game. It can be made into disks for game machines or downloaded to be played on computers. It's called Pearly Gates. You have a line of people waiting to get into the pearly gates. Your hero, Gabe, has to run the obstacle course. Each time he passes an obstacle, the person in front of the line moves one step closer to the pearly gates. When he finishes his course, someone will be standing in front of the open gates, a halo will come down on their head and they will enter. Then Gabe will go on to get the next person in line to the gates. The obstacle course is changed for each game." Les finished his explanation and looked up to see a lot of people listening. He grinned.

"I like it," said Jacob. "Hurry up and finish it up so we can get it into production."

"Yes, Sir, I'll do my best," agreed Les.

Lily and the ladies came back downstairs. Elaine was carrying Lucky. She was talking to him like he could understand every word she said. Who knows, maybe he could. He didn't take his eyes off of her. Lily smiled at Les and went to fix Lucky a bottle. When she walked past Les, he took her hand and pulled her to a stop.

"Lily, this is my granddad, Jacob Porter. Granddad, this is Lily."

Jacob was standing and he pulled Lily into a hug. "I'm happy to meet you, Lily. Welcome to the family. Lily hugged him back.

"I'm happy to meet you, too. I hope we get to see a lot of you all. Lucky needs to know all of you while he is growing up," she said.

"I'll make sure of it," assured Jacob with a smile.

"I had better get his bottle while he is being nice," said Lily with a glance over to where Lucky was being entertained by his new relatives.

There was soon a group sitting around the table with Les, Doug, and Jacob All of their friends were excited to be in the company of the Jacob Porter. They could live for months off the bragging rights.

The ladies were in the living room gathered around Elaine and Mallory. They were all talking excitedly back and forth. There was no class distinction in this group. They were all being treated just like friends and neighbors.

Elaine turned to Lily as she sat giving Lucky his bottle.

"How did you and Les meet?" she asked.

"He was Love's Answer shown to me by a magic mirror," responded Lily.

THE END

ABOUT THE AUTHOR

Betty McLain

With five children, ten grandchildren and six great-grandchildren, I have a very busy life, but reading and writing have always been a very large and enjoyable part of my life. I have been writing since I was very young. I kept notebooks with my stories in them private. I didn't share them with anyone. They were all handwritten because I was unable to type. We lived in the country, and I had to do most of my writing at night. My days were busy helping with my brothers and sister. I also helped Mom with the garden and canning food for our family. Even though I was tired, I still managed to get my thoughts down on paper at night.

When I married and began raising my family, I continued writing my stories while helping my children through school and into their own lives and families. My sister was the only one to read my stories. She was very encouraging. When my youngest daughter started college, I decided to go to college myself. I had taken my GED at an earlier date and only had to take a class to pass my college entrance tests. I passed with flying colors and even managed to get a partial scholarship. I took computer classes to learn typing. The English language and literature classes helped me to polish my stories.

I found public speaking was not for me. I was much more comfortable with the written word but researching and writing the speeches was helpful. I could use information to build a story. I still managed to put my own spin on the essays.

I finished college with an associate degree and a 3.4 GPA. I won several awards, including President's List, Dean's List, and Faculty List. The school experience helped me gain more confidence in my writing. I want to thank my English teacher in college for giving me more confidence in my writing by telling me that I had a good imagination. She said I told an interesting story. My daughter, who is a very good writer and has books of her own published, convinced me to have some of my stories published. She used her experience self-publishing to publish my stories them for me. The first time I held one of my books in my hands and looked at my name on it as author, I was so proud. They were very well received. This was encouragement enough to convince me to continue writing and publishing. I have been building my library of books written by Betty McLain since then. I also wrote and illustrated several children's books.

Being able to type my stories opened up a whole new world for me. Having access to a computer helped me to look up anything I needed to know and expanded my ability to keep writing my books. Joining Facebook and making friends all over the world expanded my outlook considerably. I was able to understand many different lifestyles and incorporate them in my ideas.

I have heard the saying, "Watch out what you say, and don't make the writer mad, you may end up in a book being eliminated." It is true. All of life is there to stimulate your imagination. It is fun to sit and think about how a thought can be changed to develop a story and to watch the story develop and come alive in your mind. When I get started, the stories almost write themselves; I just have to get all of it down as I think it before it is gone.

I love knowing the stories I have written are being read and enjoyed by others. It is awe-inspiring to look at the books and think, "I wrote that."

I look forward to many more years of putting my stories out there and hope the people reading my books are looking forward to reading them as much.